THE WRANGLER'S
READY-MADE FAMILY

LACY WILLIAMS

1

Winter 1909

Susie Crowell née White gritted her teeth as she was jostled by another lurch of the stagecoach.

Two-year-old Carrie moved in her sleep, and Susie soothed her by rubbing her thumb at the girl's temple. She was nestled against Susie on the narrow bench seat. Here was one good thing about Susie's protruding, nine-months-pregnant stomach. It made a perfect pillow for Carrie's head.

Even as Susie thought it, the baby inside her kicked against the spot where Carrie rested. Her little one was restless. Almost as restless as Susie had grown over the last few days.

Her time was close. She wouldn't be on this stage otherwise.

It was snowing and had been for most of the morning, which made for a pretty landscape in the hilly Montana countryside. Susie didn't know the name of the mountains in the distance, but they reminded her of Bear Creek. Of home.

While the scenery outside the stage was snow-covered and beautiful, inside was stuffy enough that Susie had thrown aside the scratchy woolen blanket the driver had given her earlier.

The small space was surprisingly crowded.

Susie had paid a full fare for her daughter, though Carrie wasn't able to use the entire middle seat thanks to the portly man on her other side. He was sprawled across the bench, unconcerned for anyone else. The three seats opposite were also occupied. A man who must be close to thirty and two older women had joined the stage mid-morning.

One of them—wearing an ostentatious feather in her hat—had asked where Susie's husband was. When Susie had answered "I have no husband," the old biddies had shared a judgmental look and ignored her since.

Their narrow-eyed glares had been another reminder of home. Of her sister Cecilia. Nothing Susie had ever done was good enough for Cecilia. Susie was too flirtatious. Her clothes weren't modest enough. She couldn't sit still through lessons.

The babe moved inside her, and for one moment, Susie wished that everything that had passed between her and Cecilia—the awful fight and Susie running away—had never happened. What she wouldn't give for her sister to be sitting next to her right now. "Everything is going to be all right," Cecilia would whisper. Cecilia would know what to do. She always did.

It was Susie who was stumbling blindly through after making the biggest mistake of her life.

But that was all going to change.

Her husband Roy had died three months before. She was no longer trapped in a loveless marriage.

And she had two little ones to take care of.

Susie had done everything she could to survive in the ramshackle town where her gambler of a husband had stranded them. She'd taken in laundry, washing clothes until her fingers were stained and her back ached so much that no amount of rest would set it right. She had taken in mending. She had answered letters for an older woman who was partially blind but still had many friends to correspond with. It had been hard to contain her envy. When Susie was old and gray, she would have no one.

She looked down at the dark crown of her daughter's head. She would have Carrie. And she would have this baby.

The constant ache in her lower back twinged, and she shifted in her seat, moving as slowly as she could so she wouldn't wake the toddler. As she had all day, Susie felt the gaze from the coach's sixth occupant.

She didn't look across at him.

She didn't have to. Earlier, it had taken one glance to see that he was almost as handsome as Roy had been, with fair blond hair that curled at his nape beneath the brim of his hat and sharp blue eyes that seemed to miss nothing.

He hadn't smiled once during this endless journey. He was pale and quiet, and she imagined she had seen the same judgment in his gaze that she had received from the two older women.

He watched her a lot.

While the Susie of three years ago would've preened under his interest, now she only grew uncomfortable.

She'd misjudged Roy in a spectacular fashion. She'd thought the sharp way he had gazed at her meant he'd found her captivating. She'd blossomed under his pointed attention.

But Roy had only wanted her body. He hadn't been interested in knowing her. Not really. Not even after she'd convinced him to do right and marry her.

Since she'd met him, Susie had made one bad choice after another. She'd compounded her sins when she'd run away from home. And she'd paid dearly.

Now, she was finally free. And she had no desire to attract attention from any man.

Besides, she knew what she looked like. Who would be interested in *this*?

Before she had birthed Carrie, she'd prided herself on her looks. But simple survival had cost her deeply. Her skin was gray. She no longer had natural roses in her cheeks. Her hair was dull and lifeless, pulled back simply to keep it away from grabby toddler fingers. She had sewn this dress when she had been pregnant with Carrie. It was worn, and the hem was frayed.

Susie felt as frayed as the dress.

If she could just make it to her friend Hannah's home, everything would be all right. Hannah had sent a letter inviting Susie to come. Susie hadn't realized how taxing the journey would be.

She'd left everything behind. She had no house, no belongings save what she had packed in a trunk. No job to support herself. Hannah was her only hope for a fresh start.

If she could survive this awful leg of the stage route.

The ruts in the terrible road must've grown worse, because the coach seemed to sway and lurch every other second.

Susie glanced out the window, but falling snow obscured everything. How much farther was the town of Keller? Surely they were almost there.

At that moment, the stage jerked and shuddered. Susie reached out, trying to find anything that she could use to steady herself. But the stage careened before she could get a grip on anything.

Carrie came awake with a cry, and Susie clasped her close, trying to shield her small body.

The stagecoach went off kilter and then crashed with a loud sound of splintering wood.

GIL HART HAD BEEN WATCHING the pregnant woman all day.

Every time he sensed himself on the verge of a coughing fit, he examined another aspect of her and breathed as slowly as he could.

Her hands were chapped and work-roughened. But they were also tender when she smoothed back a strand of hair from her little girl's forehead.

Her eyes were dark brown. They'd flashed fire when she glared at him—the only time she'd looked at him all day. But the lashes framing her eyes were long and elegant and made her appear mysterious somehow.

Her shoes were faded, the leather scuffed. Either

her feet constantly hurt, or her back did, because she moved her feet often, shifting them this way or that.

Her dress was worn and patched.

Her mouth only smiled at her daughter.

Her chin was surprisingly expressive.

On and on it had gone.

He couldn't help it.

It was better to stave off his cough. Because one cough turned into two which turned into a coughing fit that would keep going until it stole his breath.

And he would prefer to keep breathing, for as long as he could manage.

Which wouldn't be much longer, according to his doctor.

Since his diagnosis, he'd stopped worrying so much about what others thought of him. His time on earth was short. What did it matter if he shouldn't stare because it was rude?

He'd been born curious. And watching this pregnant woman made him more so.

In his line of work, he saw mostly men, though sometimes he encountered a lady of the night.

It was easier to focus on the cards.

He liked cards. He liked counting them. Fifty-two cards in a deck. Four suits.

Cards didn't lie.

And they didn't have unreasonable expectations.

He let that thought flit away.

Why was a woman so obviously pregnant alone on this stage? Well, not alone if you counted her daughter. How old was the tot? Two? Three?

He didn't know anything about kids.

The woman was pretty enough to draw attention, with dark hair that curled in wisps around her face.

When the little girl moved, shifting in her sleep, her mother helped her settle with a brush of her fingers across the girl's arm.

How did she do that? She seemed to anticipate the child's needs.

They'd stopped for lunch at a cafe in a town whose name he didn't remember. He'd watched the young mother pass bite-sized pieces of food to her daughter and help her drink from a mug.

The woman herself had barely eaten. Instead, she'd wrapped most of the overpriced lunch in a handkerchief and tucked it in her carpetbag. Why had she done that? Another question to distract him.

She'd kept the little girl busy with a game of *eye spy* and spent hours pointing out interesting things from the stage window. A hawk. A squirrel. A funny-shaped tree.

And then she'd coaxed the little one to sleep, humming under her breath until the child's eyes had fluttered closed.

He'd felt twitchy watching the intimate moment.

Where else was he supposed to look? The over-weight man in the bowler hat sitting across from him had tipped his head back and was snoring.

The two biddies next to Gil had pulled out some kind of knitting project and were whispering to each other.

He was bored.

What he really wanted was a deck of cards.

When the dark-haired beauty glared at him again, he thought better of watching her any more.

He thought back to the last game he'd played two nights before. He replayed the first draw in his mind's eye. He'd had a pair of sixes—

Suddenly, the stagecoach made a horrendous cracking sound and tilted precariously. Gravity pushed Gil further into his seat as Bowler Hat Man woke with a grunt. He caught on immediately and reached for the leather handle above his window.

The woman across from Gil was slower to react. She reached for the handle over her head but missed it in the lurching of the stage. She was nearly thrown to the floor. She would've been, if Gil hadn't reached out and braced her with a hand to her knee.

In the chaos of raised voices, she swatted his hand away.

Had she even realized he'd helped her?

The stage came to a stop.

The little girl had woken with a startled cry, and

the woman held the tot close and pressed her cheek against the girl's. She was clinging to the seat to keep from sliding to the floor.

The child sobbed in her mother's arms.

The two older women were shrieking and wailing by the time the driver wrenched the door open.

He helped Bowler Hat Man out. Gil was quick to jump out after and turned back to help the two older women, who were scrambling after him.

He only got a brief glimpse of the shattered stage wheel and the visible crack in the axle as he passed the women off to the driver.

He reached back into the stagecoach. "Let me help you."

But the woman shook her head. She braced with one hand and clung to her daughter with the other as she slid across the bench seat.

With almost everyone safely out, the driver had moved to settle the horses in their traces. The four animals had been spooked by the crash and were prancing in place. Every movement caused the stagecoach to jostle, and Gil worried that the horses would take off and the woman would be thrown around inside the stagecoach—or even thrown out of it.

"Take my hand," he told her.

She shot him a look of seething anger and refused his outstretched hand.

"I'll manage on my own." Her voice was sweet but determined, and he wanted to shake her.

He glanced to the side, where the driver was working to unharness the horses. The man was fumbling with one of the leather straps.

The horses pulled, and the stagecoach jerked another inch.

The woman was yanked off-balance and worked to set her feet again. She was within reach now, and he didn't give her a choice. He captured her elbow, tugging her toward him at the same moment the stagecoach shuddered and moved.

She cried out and twisted, but it worked in his favor because she was swept into his arms. He whisked her and her daughter out of the stagecoach and away from danger.

The driver jumped back as the horses broke away from the last leather strap. They cantered several dozen yards before they stopped, one shaking its head, mane flying, while the others stomped in agitation.

Gil still held onto the woman, though she was struggling and clearly wanted down.

He set her feet on the ground. At that moment, the little girl reached out from where she was safely nestled in her mother's arms and patted his cheek.

He froze. The woman froze too.

He stood entirely too close. Her eyes were wide, and in them he read a mix of latent fear and uncertainty.

She jerked away, quickly walking until several yards separated them.

"You're welcome," he said.

Her chin came up, her lips pinched in a stubborn line. There was no *thank you*.

No. No, no, *no.*

Susie wanted to scream, but she was conscious of her young daughter clinging to her hand and listening intently. Carrie, normally a curious child, was silent and tearful. Her grip on Susie's hand was so tight it pinched, as if she were afraid of being ripped away from Susie by force.

Susie knew how she felt.

She was still shaken after the stagecoach crash. Still trying to hide the tremors that rattled her so Carrie wouldn't sense her fear. After being manhandled out of the conveyance, she wanted a private place to recover and calm down.

She wasn't going to get it.

"It's five miles to the nearest town," the stagecoach driver said.

The passengers were gathered around him in the blowing snow. Susie had angled herself so the coach was behind her. She didn't want to look at it.

"I can ride a horse," she said firmly. "I grew up on a ranch. Carrie and I can ride with someone else if that will help."

The two older women whispered behind gloved hands.

She didn't care what they thought of her. She just wanted to reach the safety of Hannah's home.

The driver shook his head. "One of the horses is lame. There won't be enough room for everybody. Two people will need to stay behind."

"Why shouldn't it be the two men?" Her words seemed to get lost in a swirl of snow. Had the storm worsened? The wind cut through the layers of her dress and coat. She clutched Carrie a little closer.

The stranger who'd whisked her off the stagecoach stood to her left. She was intent on ignoring him, but his presence spread larger than the man himself, and she couldn't quite manage it. Was he angry she'd suggested he stay behind?

But it was the portly man in a bowler hat who spoke. "I have a heart condition, madam. I cannot be expected to remain here."

"I can't stay," one of the older women said. "Neither can my sister." Her voice carried a false tremulous note, as if she wanted everyone to feel sorry for her.

The driver sighed. Susie knew their situation wasn't his fault—who could've expected the wheel to break like that?—but if the man would take charge, everyone would listen. Her adoptive father Oscar would've. He'd have everybody halfway to town by now instead of standing in the snow arguing.

"Nobody has to stay out in the open," the driver said, raising his voice to be heard above the arguing voices. Everyone went quiet.

"See that group of trees yonder?" He pointed off to the west, where the landscape became more hilly. "A coupla years ago, I had to shelter from a real bad thunderstorm. Just behind that grove is a rocky ridge. There's a cave there. Plenty big for two or three people. I'll come back with a wagon and what help I can find."

More arguing broke out. The trees the driver had indicated had to be a half mile away at least. Who knew how far beyond that was the cave?

The driver stopped listening. He walked back to the stagecoach and used the front wheel as a stair to boost himself up. He pulled a small satchel from beneath the seat he'd previously occupied.

"There's flint and tinder in here. Some first aid supplies if you need them." He held up the bag and then set it on the ground.

Who was he talking to? No decision had been made about who was going and who was staying.

A hacking cough escaped the tall stranger, startling Susie.

Carrie must've been startled, too, because she began sobbing. "Mama!" she cried.

Susie lifted her daughter into her arms—no small feat with her belly in the way—and stepped away from him. What a terrible sound, that cough.

Her distraction had cost her. The group wasn't arguing anymore. The two older women had rushed toward the horses. The portly man followed.

"Wait!" Susie cried out.

By the time she'd gathered the front of her skirt, juggling Carrie in her arms, and gotten moving, one of the women and the portly gentleman were already mounted on their bareback rides.

The stranger was still coughing, now bent over with a hand on his knee.

Susie kept moving, but she could see she was too late. Were they really going to leave her out here? With a small child? Alone with a man she'd never met before today?

"Stop!" she shouted.

But the driver boosted the second woman onto the third—and last—horse and clambered up behind her.

"At least take my daughter!" she called out. "Take her to Hannah Cahill. Please!"

"No!" Carrie shrieked. Her tiny arms banded around Susie's neck in a chokehold.

Maybe the blowing wind snatched her voice. Maybe the driver's sense of self-preservation was stronger than his compassion.

Whatever the case, he shouted, "Hiyah!" and his horse took off. The others followed, even the supposedly lame horse.

Leaving Susie and her daughter abandoned in a snowstorm.

She stood shaking, her arms around Carrie. This couldn't be happening. This had to be a dream. A terrible nightmare.

But no matter how many times she blinked, the same snowy landscape remained.

She turned back to the stagecoach, desperate— for what, she didn't know.

The stranger was at the coach. She couldn't see his upper body as he leaned almost inside the conveyance. He'd stopped coughing.

She didn't want to be trapped out here with him. What if he was a criminal?

He emerged from the coach with a folded bundle that must be the blankets they'd used. He also carried a small satchel and a bulkier bag that clanked when he moved. And her carpetbag.

"That's mine," she called out sharply.

He arched one brow. "I know."

"I'd appreciate it if you wouldn't touch—"

"I thought I'd carry it for you," he interrupted. "You seem to have your hands full."

Of all the arrogant—

He started walking in the direction of the grove the driver had pointed out.

"I'm not going to sit in a cave with you." If he was a killer, he'd have a handy place to hide her body. Why make it easy on him?

"Suit yourself," he called over his shoulder. "You and your little one will turn into blocks of ice in a few hours."

She only resisted the urge to scream by clamping down on her back teeth.

He kept walking.

Carrie sniffled, raising her head from Susie's shoulder. "I no wanna be ice."

Heart thrumming, Susie stared into her daughter's face.

Carrie watched her with wide, dark eyes. Trusting eyes. Sometimes, like now, Susie was reminded of her younger sister Velma when the girl had been small.

Susie had been eight when Velma was born. Mama had died soon after. Susie and her older sister Cecilia had done their best to raise Velma without much help from their worthless stepfather. It had been almost a year before Sarah and Oscar had come along and adopted them. A year of eating only half a meal so that Velma would have food to fill her belly. Of rocking her sister to sleep, not knowing whether they'd have a roof over their heads come morning.

All that time, Velma had gazed at Susie and Cecilia just like this. With absolute trust.

And Susie was reminded of the night her daughter had been born. She'd stared into the tiny, red face and promised she would always protect Carrie.

Now, she swallowed back her own fear and trepidation and made herself smile, just like she had for Velma all those years ago. "Guess what, darling? We're going to have an adventure. Just like in a storybook."

Carrie sniffled once more, her lips curving in a smile.

"Everything is going to be all right."

She was going to make it so. Even if that meant passing a few hours in the presence of a stranger. She had a derringer in her coat pocket. If he tried anything untoward, she'd use it.

Everything is going to be all right.

The baby inside her kicked as if in agreement.

And Susie followed the stranger to find a cave.

ONCE GIL HAD DETERMINED the woman was following him, he slowed his steps to let her catch up.

But she kept a good distance between them, as if she didn't want him close.

That was fine with him. He was embarrassed that she'd witnessed his coughing fit. His lungs still burned from it. That and the cold.

Her daughter was bundled on her shoulder, the girl's face tucked into the woman's neck for warmth.

He tried to judge the distance to the trees. It couldn't be much longer now.

The woman was muttering.

"Did you say something?" he asked.

"I said—" She cut herself off and pressed a gloved hand over her daughter's ear. "I can't believe those scoundrels left us out here."

She glared at him as if he'd been one of the riders instead of being marooned in a snowstorm along with her.

He shrugged. He'd had occasion to see human nature at its worst. A man on a losing streak was a dangerous thing. Tempers were ugly, and adding alcohol to the mix meant sometimes that ugliness showed.

He'd made it a practice to stay out of those situations.

But even he was a little surprised that the driver had left a helpless pregnant woman behind. It wasn't right.

He'd have something to say to the man when they got back to civilization, but there was nothing to do but make the best of it now.

Was she going to be standoffish the entire time?

Maybe she was just shy.

"Name's Gilbert Hart," he said. "You can call me Gil. I figure if we're going to be stuck out here for a day or two, you might want to know my name."

"Surely it won't be that long." She sounded dismayed.

"Maybe not, if your husband gets wind that you're out here."

He'd hoped to win a smile, but if anything, her frown grew fiercer. Seemed like she was stomping, though he couldn't be sure in the snow.

"My husband is dead," she said finally. Her words were matter-of-fact. Almost angry. "But my friend Hannah is expecting us, and she'll bring the law down on you if I don't show up in town."

He snorted. Then took another look at her. "Wait a minute. Do you really think I'm gonna hurt you?"

She had the grace to blush, but her chin rose stubbornly. "We don't know each other."

He glanced at the snow blowing around them. "We're gonna get to know each other real quick. Might go easier if you tell me your name."

"Susie Crowell," she said grudgingly. "And this is Carrie."

She shifted the little girl in her arms. The tyke must be heavy, but her mama hadn't put her down once. He would've offered to trade her the blankets and carry the girl himself, but she'd made it clear she didn't trust him.

"Do you really think it'll be tomorrow before someone comes for us?" she asked.

Tomorrow might be wishful thinking. Those city folks wouldn't be able to travel very fast riding bareback like they were.

"The driver said it was five miles to town. As long as the weather lets up, they could be back tomorrow."

But the clouds seemed to almost press toward the ground, heavy with more snow.

She had followed his upward gaze, and now her face crumpled a little before she smoothed out her expression.

She had courage, that was for sure. She hadn't wilted like some hothouse flower. And pretty too. It was a shame about her husband.

They reached the first of the trees, and the ground became rockier as it rose up a slight hill. He had to watch his step, but it was hard in the snow. It must be doubly difficult for her, carrying the child and with her girth in the way.

She was huffing with exertion, though she was trying to hide it, turning her head slightly away from him. They had to be close, didn't they?

He squinted, trying to see through the falling snow and the trees ahead. Where was the ridge the driver had promised they'd see?

Susie seemed to shudder, letting out a pained breath.

He shifted the blankets and bags he carried to his left arm. "I can carry your girl. Give you a break."

The girl turned her head so she was looking at him. She had a hand tucked under her chin. She was a cute little thing, though he imagined he saw an echo of Susie's distrust in her expression.

"I can manage." The words came out between huffs.

He was only trying to be helpful, but she glared at him as if he had offered to make a stew out of her daughter instead. Her face was pale, her eyes a little wild.

They trudged along in silence until her breathing grew labored.

"Do you need to stop and rest?"

She shook her head tightly.

Fine.

The trees seemed to thin just ahead, and he lengthened his stride. The wind blew fiercer here.

Like it was skirting the base of a mountain.

He left Susie to follow and pushed past the last few trees. There was a rock outcropping.

And a dark gash against the landscape. It was smaller than he'd expected.

But they'd found the cave.

3

G il had recognized his companion's silent dismay as they approached the cave. But Susie kept her disappointment to a frown. Probably for her daughter's sake.

The entrance was a crawl-space, which they would have to crawl on hands and knees to pass through.

She'd readily allowed him to go inside first to explore it. When he called for her to follow, she did, moving slowly. It couldn't be easy for her, not while she still carried her baby inside. The little girl, Carrie, walked in front of her, Susie prodding her with a hand at her back. They arrived and scrambled to sit against the wall.

From inside the cave, dim light filtered through the opening and illuminated the small space.

It was barely big enough for the three of them to lie down side-by-side. Neither of the adults could stand, thanks to the low ceiling. It was dirty and cramped.

On the other hand, though the air inside the cave was damp, it was warmer than the chilly wind outside. For the first time since they'd been ejected from the broken stagecoach, the icy fire in his lungs abated. He inhaled a slow, deep breath. Then one more.

Susie and Carrie were still huddled in their coats, but the space would heat up even more once he got a fire going.

She was looking around distastefully when he passed her one of the blankets. He found a worn cooking pot in the bag the driver had pressed on him and set it aside. They might need to melt snow unless there was some kind of stream nearby.

Susie put the blanket on the ground and pulled Carrie close to sit on it. She cupped her hands over the girl's ears. "Are you sure there aren't any wild animals in here?"

It was sweet how she tried to protect her daughter.

"I don't see any scat. Do you?" It was impossible to make out any tracks in the rocky ground. He motioned to the back of the cave. "It seems to keep going, but the space is so small, only a barn cat could make it through there."

She pulled a face.

"If there's anything back there, they'll want to stay as far away from us as they can."

She didn't look reassured.

"Mama." Carrie tugged on her sleeve. "I'm hungry."

He edged toward the crawlspace. "The first order of business is to build a fire," he said. "I'll scout around for some wood."

Susie nodded absently. He'd put her carpetbag near the cave wall, out of their way. Now when she twisted her body to reach for it, she inhaled sharply and tensed up. Like she was in pain.

He stopped and turned back. "You all right?"

She pressed one hand against her belly and exhaled. But she kept her head down and didn't look at him.

Fissures of unease rose up his spine.

She exhaled again, and her muscles unclenched. "I'm fine." This time when she reached for the bag, she got it. She unclasped it and reached inside.

Carrie seemed nonplussed, having stepped away from her mama to touch one of the rock walls that surrounded them.

"You sure?" he asked Susie. He was no stranger to pain. And it sure looked like she'd experienced it.

"I'm fine," she repeated quietly.

Maybe it had been a cramp from walking so far. He didn't know anything about pregnant women or what plagued them. And maybe it wasn't polite to think so, but she was so big that he had to wonder whether she was close to giving birth.

That was a thought to strike fear in his heart.

But he had to focus on their survival. "I'll be right back."

She still refused to look at him as he scooted out of the cave.

Back into the woods he went. His lungs protested being forced to bear the cold again, and he found himself hunched over and coughing so deeply that he scared a pair of crows from their roost high in a tree. They flew away with angry-sounding *caw caws* aimed in his direction.

He braced one hand against a stubby evergreen, struggling for breath until his coughing fit finally stopped. He stood with his head hanging low, counting breaths.

He knew the consumption was going to steal his life. But Susie and her daughter were going to be in a world of hurt if he expired today.

He needed to find as much wood as he could, as quickly as he could, and then stay inside the cave.

He opened his eyes—he hadn't even realized he'd closed them—and saw that his boots had scuffed away the top layer of snow and revealed a cache of yellowed, needle-like leaves. The memory was faint, but as a boy he'd read plenty of dime novels about the Wild West. Didn't folks use pine needles like these to get a fire started?

He stuffed as many as he could inside his coat pockets.

The light on this side of the mountain was fading, another reason he needed to work fast. Not far from the evergreen, he stumbled across a slender tree that must've fallen a season or two past. It lay on its side, roots exposed. Its branches were brittle enough that he could break them off with a hard stomp from his boot. But the wood didn't seem rotted, which meant it would be perfect for his needs.

He broke it up and carted three armfuls of wood to the cave, piling them inside the mouth without crawling inside. When his lungs threatened to collapse, he abandoned the task for the time being and crawled inside.

Carrie was munching on a piece of bread and one of cheese. At least, he thought that's what it was. With the light dimming outside, the cave was growing even darker.

Near the mouth of the cave, he scooped away gravel and dirt to make a depression in the ground for their fire. He put it close to one wall, so they'd have room to scoot past it if they needed to leave the cave.

Carrie was chattering to her mama as he forced his numb fingers to stack twigs and pile evergreen needles beneath them. A sudden worry crept into his head.

"Was there really flint and tinder in the driver's satchel?" he asked over his shoulder.

Susie murmured something to Carrie, and by the time he'd turned his head, the little girl had brought him the steel striker and flint and a tiny gob of cotton batting.

"Thank you," he told her.

He had the fire crackling in minutes. It was smoky, thanks to the snowy, wet wood. But fortunately, the smoke made its way out of the cave instead of filling the interior. And the firelight provided enough illumination to see that Susie had spread out more of the blankets. She sat on one, and there was room for her to lie down and stretch out. A napkin lay across her knee, one that he recognized from the stop they'd made for the noon meal.

He scoured his memory but couldn't remember what Susie had eaten earlier.

"Did you get enough to eat?" he asked.

She folded up the napkin, giving the simple task too much concentration. "I'm fine."

Fine. He had a sense she'd be "fine" for the duration. It wasn't an answer. And he didn't believe her. Not this time. Not when he sensed she'd given Carrie all the leftovers from the noon meal.

He fed another stick into the fire, then judged it big enough that he added a small log.

Carrie was sitting half-hidden behind her mama, playing with a rag doll.

Gil left the fire for now and sat against the opposite wall. With his legs outstretched, he could touch Susie's knee with his toe if he wanted. The space wasn't ideal, but it was what they had, and it was much better than being out in the elements.

He rustled in his own satchel and brought out the paper-wrapped parcel he'd stashed there earlier. He'd guessed that his body wouldn't be happy about the days of travel and the fact that he'd be too exhausted once they'd reached Keller to want to leave his hotel room and find food. He'd bought a second lunch and asked the cook to wrap it up for him.

Planning for his future self's laziness had paid off.

Susie watched him furtively as he lifted the sandwich and broke it in half. When he lifted one half, her eyes darted away.

Until he extended it to her. "Have some."

Her gaze landed on him, narrow-eyed and wary. "That's yours."

"It'd be a shame for you to pass the night hungry. It's probably safe to assume help isn't coming until morning." If then.

Her gaze on the sandwich was intent and hungry. But then she dropped her eyes. "We don't know how long it'll be," she whispered. "You might want it later."

He sighed, exasperated. "What I want is for you to quit arguing and eat this."

She had to be hungry. It was admirable that she'd taken care of her child before her own needs, but there was no reason for her to go hungry. Not yet, anyway.

SUSIE'S HAND was shaking as she took the food from Gil. She prayed he didn't notice.

Her stomach gnawed with hunger, her mouth moistening as her brain registered the scent of bread and meat.

She summoned all the humility she could muster. "Thank you, Mr. Hart."

"I think if we're going to get through the next day or so together, you'd better call me Gil."

It felt too intimate. She cut her gaze to the side. When she bit into the sandwich, flavor exploded over her tongue.

"Mama!"

She'd never been so grateful for an interruption from Carrie. She was beginning to think that Gil saw too much.

"What kinda an'mals live inna cave?" Carrie asked.

"Bats," Gil offered when Susie hesitated for too long.

Susie wrinkled her nose. She didn't want to think about bats flying out from that tiny, dark space in the back of the cave. She didn't want to think about any of it.

Carrie looked to Susie for approval, then once she'd received it, toddled over to Gil. "Whatsa bat?"

The man looked stumped for a moment and then tried to describe the mammal. Only Carrie interrupted with her usual curious questions.

And Susie let her.

Not only because she wanted a moment of peace to devour the half-sandwich—who was she kidding? It was gone in less than a moment. But because she needed a breath to compose herself.

It wasn't until Mr. Hart had been gone for several minutes and time seemed to stretch interminably that Susie realized how very reliant she was on his charity.

What if he didn't come back?

She could struggle through the snow to find firewood, but what would she do with Carrie? Expose her to the elements?

What if no one came back for them?

What had she done, hiking all the way out here, even further from civilization than the stagecoach on a lonely road?

She'd gotten herself worked up into a panic by the time he returned with his firewood. She'd been so relieved to see him that she'd nearly burst into tears and had turned her face away lest he see.

After everything that had happened with Roy, she'd promised herself that she would never find herself reliant on another man. She would do whatever she had to do to secure her children's future, to keep them safe and well-fed.

But she'd never prepared for a wilderness blizzard.

And she *did* need Mr. Hart, no matter how much she wished things were different.

She thought about how rude she'd been back at the stagecoach—no matter that she'd been shaken from the accident and angry about being abandoned out there. And how coldly she'd treated Mr. Hart since.

If she wanted to secure his help during the hours they would be trapped together out here, she must put on a more pleasant demeanor. Her life, Carrie's life, even her unborn baby's life, depended on it.

Her own distaste couldn't be a factor.

"How come it's snowin' so much?" asked Carrie.

It wasn't clear who the question was addressed to. The child was walking from Gil to Susie but looking at neither of them.

She answered. She didn't want Gil to grow annoyed with Carrie. "It just is, sweetie."

He glanced at the cave entrance, though it had grown dark and no light came through.

"I don't suppose you're much of a hunter," he said.

It took a moment for her to realize he was teasing.

Another moment, and her memories presented her with a visual of Papa coming through the door with a fat Christmas turkey in hand. He was an excellent hunter and supplemented the family's diet with game.

She couldn't think about home. It hurt too much.

She swallowed hard.

"One of my uncles taught me to make a snare trap," she said. "If you have any twine, maybe I can describe it to you." Though she had no idea whether any animals would be out in a snowstorm like this.

She shifted, her hip aching from sitting on the rocky ground. And when she did, the muscles of her stomach contracted in a labor pain.

She tried not to show it. She breathed shallowly for a few seconds until it passed.

That was the second one today. The first had been during their hike from the stagecoach. She'd written it off as a fluke because of the effort of walking and carrying her daughter.

But two pains...

She was not in labor. This had to be something else.

But her body remembered the pains from when she'd given birth to Carrie, and these felt the same.

It was too early. At least a week early, if she'd counted the months right.

The pains had been far apart.

They could go away.

Mama had given birth to three children, and Susie knew that sometimes she would have phantom birth pains in the weeks before she gave birth. This could be the very same.

She ignored the thought that she hadn't had any phantom pains with Carrie.

She wasn't giving birth in this dirty, dank cave.

She distracted herself by readying Carrie for bed. Carrie hummed an unrecognizable tune as Susie used a handkerchief to wipe off her face.

"I'm not sleepy," the girl said when Susie asked her to lie down.

And then she promptly yawned so big that she rocked back on her heels.

"Well, I am." Susie ignored the man watching and

stretched her arms over her head. Pretended that she wasn't terrified to be sleeping in a cave with a complete stranger in the wilderness.

Her mother would've had a conniption to see her out here. That thought had her firming her lips stubbornly. This was Susie's life. And Mama didn't get a say. Not anymore.

She managed to get Carrie to lie down beside her and began the nightly ritual of singing a song she could barely remember her birth mother singing in her faintest memories. She was aware of Gil where he knelt over the fire, stoking it. He was careful not to look at her, but she knew he was listening.

Heat filled her cheeks. She didn't have the best voice, but this was the only way to get Carrie to sleep.

After the song, Carrie started a rambling, disjointed prayer.

Susie let her mind wander. She didn't know what to make of the man. His clothing reminded her of how Roy used to dress. Her late husband favored dark suits and fancy tooled boots. So did Gil.

It didn't mean anything.

She knew plenty of men who liked to dress in fine suits who weren't gamblers.

Like Roy, Gil was handsome. The firelight turned his skin golden and made his eyes seem dark and fathomless.

Before she had really known him, she thought Roy the finest specimen of a man. Now she knew how good looks could hide a man's true nature. As far as she was concerned, good looks were a strike against him.

He coughed, reaching in his pocket for a handkerchief. She'd heard him cough several times today and wondered whether he might be sick. She must've made some noise because he glanced at her, dabbing his mouth once more. He nodded once, and heat filled her face at being caught staring.

"It's consumption," he said. He sounded almost resigned. "Doctors say it's not contagious."

Carrie had gone silent, Susie realized too late.

"What's cermsupton?"

Susie shushed her, her brain scrambling for an explanation that would satisfy her curious daughter and not offend Gil.

But it was he who spoke next, his words quiet. "It means that sometimes I can't stop coughing. Sometimes I can't breathe."

Susie felt a pang of compassion. There had been plenty of days in her marriage that she had felt as if she couldn't breathe. Hers hadn't been a physical ailment, but the feeling of being trapped in a life that she had never expected and didn't want had seemed suffocating.

But knowing one was actually suffocating?

She stifled the shudder. How awful.

Carrie bowed her head again, her hands folded beneath her chin. "Please be with Mr. Gil and his cermsupton. Make him better."

Susie looked up at her daughter's quiet "amen." She couldn't help smiling at Carrie's pure faith. This was one thing she had done right, going back to the faith that her parents had instilled in her.

But Gil ducked his head, his face drawn as if he were in pain.

She kissed Carrie's cheek, pretending she hadn't seen. It wasn't her business. She felt almost as if she'd looked in a mirror at the Susie of three months ago. In the looking glass, she had seen a woman with absolutely no hope.

And now she had a kernel. If she could get to Keller. To Hannah.

She just had to survive until then.

She laid close to Carrie and closed her eyes. The little girl would fall asleep faster if Susie pretended to be asleep too.

But behind her closed eyes, she couldn't forget the image of the man and his silent pain.

4

Gil dozed on and off all night, stoking the fire when it needed stoking.

The cave remained at a comfortable temperature, though he woke several times when one of his companions rolled over. Once, Carrie murmured something unintelligible in her sleep.

Dawn's light was streaming in the mouth of the cave when he opened his eyes. What had woken him?

A soft gasp tickled his memory. He recognized the familiar sound. That's what had brought him to awareness.

He turned to see Susie, who was curled toward him, the blanket thrown off. Carrie must be snug against her back. Susie's hands were clenched into fists pressing against her stomach. Her face was drawn in pain that galvanized him into action.

He rolled to his knees, shuffling toward her in the tight space.

"What's the matter?"

She was panting through clenched teeth, and for one frightening moment he wondered if she would even be able to answer him.

And then she let out a gust of breath, and he was startled to see that she was blinking away tears.

"I-I'm fine." But her eyes slid to the side, and he had enough experience with reading tells to know she was lying.

He'd seen her freeze up once yesterday. Like she'd been in pain, though it had passed quickly. He'd never spent time with a woman this close to giving birth before, but what else could it be? "You're having your baby, aren't you?"

Her mouth thinned to a stubborn line. "I've got a few days yet."

She was denying it? He'd heard three or four of those gasps during the night but had assumed she was sleeping. If not for the faint light coming from the cave's entrance, he'd still believe that.

"I'm not having my baby in this cave," she said.

He didn't know much about birthing babies, but he was pretty sure women didn't get a say in when the babies came. "I don't think you're going to have much choice."

Her mouth was trembling, but when she spoke it was pure stubbornness in her voice. "The driver promised he would come back for us. Surely he'll be here soon with a-a wagon. Or sleigh. Something."

He shook his head, but she was determined to have her say.

"The pains are still far apart. They could still go away." She didn't sound as if she believed the words she was saying. But if that was what she needed to tell herself, he wasn't going to argue.

"What can I do?"

When she looked his direction, eyes blinking fast, he thought he saw her face crumple, but it happened so quickly that it was probably just a trick of the fire light.

"I don't want Carrie to be frightened. If she sees me in pain…"

Right. "I can distract her." He didn't know how exactly he would do that. Carrie was an inquisitive little thing, though. Surely he could fumble his way through it. "How much longer will she sleep?"

She shook her head slightly. "I don't know." With her head pillowed on her arm like that, she was pretty as a picture, and he told himself to back up. She didn't need him in her space.

"I'll go out and round up some more firewood."

Her eyes widened, and he rushed on, "Just in case we're stuck here for a few more hours. That way I can get right back, and I won't have to leave you again."

She might believe that help was coming, but if it had snowed all night, the trail might be impassable.

He was aiming to ask her whether she wanted him to fetch some snow to melt for water when he felt the familiar tickle at the back of his throat. He turned so he was in profile to her and breathed deeply through his nose as he stared at the flickering light on the cave walls. He counted to ten, then twenty, as he tried to stifle the need to cough. The last thing he wanted to do was wake up Carrie. A coughing fit would echo off the walls in here.

And what if he couldn't stop?

When the tightness in his chest finally passed, he worked to button up his coat. His fingers fumbled with the task, and his face flamed.

He didn't particularly like having a witness to how weak he was.

He could sense her watching him. He kept his head down, eyes focused on his fingers. "Don't worry. It's not contagious."

"Are you all right?"

He shook his head slightly. He wasn't. And he wouldn't be ever again. Every time he thought he had settled the matter, his heart reminded him that he still had a whole lot of living that he wanted to do.

But his want was irrelevant.

He finished with his coat and shifted so he was on his hands and knees to crawl outside. "I'll be back as soon as I can."

It was a blessing to stand up tall and stretch.

Birds were chirping, and the sun was peeking out from the horizon. But the snow was a blanket as high as Gil's shin. Up to his knee in the drifts—he learned that the hard way when he took a wrong step.

He struggled through the snow to the fallen log he'd found yesterday, brought two more armloads of wood. The second go-round was easier when he could follow the trail through snow that he'd already broken.

But his lungs were burning after he'd deposited the second armful just inside the cave. He straightened and scanned the landscape as he tried to steady his breathing. Snow this deep... no one would be risking his life to rescue the forsaken travelers.

They weren't getting out of there today, no matter what Susie wanted to think.

He'd saved what he could from the food he'd bought yesterday. Two apples and some dried out bread. It wouldn't last long. And he was no hunter.

He could bear the hunger pangs, but Carrie was tiny and Susie needed sustenance.

He was still thinking over the dilemma when they crawled from the cave. The little girl's hair was tousled, and she was blinking sleepily.

"She needs a private moment," Susie murmured. She took a moment to look around, and her lips pinched in concern. "That's a lot of snow."

So it was.

The decision he'd been mulling on solidified. "I'm going back to the stage," he said. "Maybe there's food that got left behind. And we might need more blankets."

Or a doctor. Too bad he wouldn't find one of those packed away in a trunk.

"Are you certain? Will you be all right in the cold?"

He hadn't told her anything about how the cold affected him, but she was smart enough to have figured it out. She'd seen him struggling for breath when they'd hiked the night before.

"I'll have to be. Anything in your trunk you want me to fetch?"

She considered him for a moment, disquiet in her eyes. "There are some baby things at the top. Just in case," she added quickly.

He nodded gravely. "Just in case."

Just in case he had to deliver a baby out in the wilderness.

SUSIE WORRIED the whole time Gil was gone, and the worry ramped up more with every passing minute.

Surely the man knew his own limitations. She'd heard of consumption, but she'd never asked detailed questions of her uncle Maxwell. Thinking of her uncle had her thinking of *all* her uncles and every male cousin. Every one of them was foolish when it came to a dare or proving their worth as a cowboy. None of them had a lick of sense.

What if Gil was the same? What if trying to get back to the stage was a mistake, some foolish male need to prove himself? What if he was too sick to make it back?

She didn't have a timepiece, but two pains had come and gone by the time the light was blocked from the cave entrance and he crawled inside.

She was so happy to see him that she could've cried. But she hid that unneeded emotion and helped him drag inside the loot he'd brought along. She distracted Carrie with her rag doll. Carrie hummed to the doll, oblivious to the adults for now.

Gil sprawled out with his legs outstretched in

front of him. His head leaned back against the cave wall as he struggled for breath.

His cheeks were red and chapped from the cold, his eyes glassy. The rattle in his breath scared her.

His pants were wet up to his knees from slogging through the deep snow. His hands were shaking until he noticed her staring. Then he fisted them on his thighs.

She scooted and reached across the floor to the pot they'd been using to melt water for drinking. She passed it to Gil, who took it silently. After a few sips, his breathing seemed to steady.

But her heart was still beating in her ears.

He'd gone through a lot to bring back supplies and fetch her things. Maybe he'd almost killed himself to do it.

When she whispered a tremulous "thank-you," he waved it off.

But she knew debts weren't so easily forgotten. Roy had once bought her a parasol when he was flush with cash. A few weeks later, there'd been a bad spell. Susie's stomach grumbled with hunger because she was pregnant with Carrie, and he'd called her ungrateful and flung the parasol across the room.

Susie couldn't afford to be indebted to anyone. Much less a fancy-pants man like Gil.

"There wasn't so much as a crumb among the luggage," he murmured.

She tried to hide her dismay by staring down at her hands. That wasn't good. There was plenty of snow to melt for water, but how long could they go without food? She worried for Carrie most of all.

But what could she do?

The day wore on, and Susie's pains began to come closer together. No matter how hard she prayed, they weren't going away. This baby was ready to be in the world, and Susie could do nothing to prevent it.

True to his word, every time a pain came upon her, Gil distracted Carrie. He'd found a square of blue chalk somewhere in the stagecoach—he hadn't said it in so many words, but she knew he'd raided all the luggage that had been left behind—and Carrie had taken great joy in drawing indecipherable sketches on the walls of the cave.

He had involved Carrie in toting pot-fulls of snow inside to fill the larger cooking pot he'd also brought back from the stage. They spent far too long melting water, but Carrie was happy and busy.

He had even told a far-fetched story about a talking baby bunny who had been lost in the woods and found several new animal friends before she got back home.

Susie didn't want to think about what she would've done if he hadn't been there. Yesterday, she'd resented his presence, and today all she felt was relief.

Late in the afternoon, she managed to get Carrie to lie down for a rest. Once her daughter was asleep, she nodded toward the cave entrance. "I'm going to stretch and pace around a little bit."

Gil shifted. "Will she"—he nodded to Carrie—"be all right if I come too?"

"Yes. I won't go far." She'd be able to see if Carrie left the cave.

He crawled out ahead of her.

She was on her hands and knees, almost free of the cave, when another pain took her. This one was so strong that she cried out.

Gil knelt in front of her and reached for her hands, clenched in the snow. She should probably be concerned about how inappropriate it was to hold hands with a man she barely knew. But as her body clamped down, starting at her stomach and radiating outward, she squeezed his hands and didn't care what was right or wrong.

The pain faded at last. Gil kept her hands and helped her stand.

When he let go, she felt a funny sense of loss. What a ninny she was.

He fell into step beside her. She wasn't moving fast, but being on her feet in the fresh air instead of sitting in that dank cave felt wonderful. The sun was already falling in the sky, and it wouldn't be long before it went behind the mountain.

Gil's boots crunched through the layers of snow. "I know you were hoping that help would arrive, but maybe it's time to admit that this baby is going to get here before that stagecoach driver does. If you'll tell me what to do, how to help, I'll do whatever you need."

She couldn't help it. Her eyes filled with tears. She blinked them back, drawing a breath to try and steady herself. Roy had rarely, if ever, cared about her needs. He hadn't even been home on the night Carrie had been born. Susie had been hopeful then, still pretending that he could change. That he would be a storybook hero. She'd shared her plans with him, anticipating the baby with diapers and tiny gowns. He hadn't cared about any of it.

Gil was practically a stranger, but he was offering his help. Even though she'd been unkind at the start of all of this.

"Give me five more minutes of pretending," she said softly.

He nodded. "Shall we pretend we met under better circumstances, then?" He made a show of stepping closer and winding her arm through his elbow. "Maybe we're taking a promenade around town."

She couldn't help the laugh that bubbled out of

her. Who would ask a woman as pregnant as she, literally on the verge of having a baby, to go for a stroll? It was such a ridiculous thought that she couldn't help the laughter, nor the bitterness that tinged it. But then another pain came upon her, and she gasped.

She stopped walking. Gil turned toward her, holding her upper arms lightly. She let her head fall forward. He was barely touching her, just his hands at her arms. But somehow she knew that if she leaned her weight on him, he wouldn't let her fall.

She tried not to whimper as the intensity of the pain grew.

And just as he had distracted Carrie earlier, he kept talking.

"I've got family back East. My father is a railroad tycoon."

So he came from money. It explained the fancy suit and well-made belongings.

"I think you would like my mother. She hosts high tea at home once a week and never seems to run out of things to talk about. She and Carrie have that in common."

Susie exhaled and laughed a little at the same time, the pain finally abating.

And she wanted to give him something of herself, so she said, "I'm afraid she comes by it naturally. My mother called me her chatterbox when I was young." She realized she was smiling up into his face.

He wore a thoughtful expression, and one corner of his mouth ticked up. She hadn't thought about her birth mother in a long time. She'd known her mother would be just as ashamed of the choices Susie had made as Mama and Cecilia were. But somehow sharing this long ago memory with him was more poignant than bittersweet.

"Are you hoping this next little one will be a chatterbox too? Perhaps your mother will extend the nickname to encompass her as well."

His words cast a shadow over her as if a cloud had blocked the sky sun. It was suddenly too much to stand this close to him. She turned away, though he kept her arm as they walked slowly forward.

"I am estranged from my family," she said stiffly.

He was silent for a moment. "That's a shame," he said finally. "I bet your mother would love to know Carrie."

He couldn't know it, because he knew nothing about her family or why she'd left. But his words were a reminder of everything she'd lost.

Mama would never know Carrie.

And Carrie would never know Papa's contagious belly laugh or have Leo, Papa and Mama's oldest, help with her homework.

Susie had been full of self-righteousness when

she'd left her family behind. And once their fears had been proved right, she was too ashamed to go back.

Cecilia was stubborn. Her sister would never forgive her.

Mama must be so disappointed, she wouldn't want…

Another pain took hold and again, Gil braced her, holding her upright with only the strength of his arms.

When it was over, tears streamed down Susie's face. Not all of them were from the physical pain.

He offered her his handkerchief. She kept her head down, not wanting him to see.

"I think your five minutes of pretending are over," he said quietly.

He was right. Whether she wanted it to happen this way or not, her baby was coming.

5

S usie panted through another labor pain. They were coming fast now. It wouldn't be much longer.

Night had fallen. Carrie had been awake for several hours after her nap but was asleep again. Susie had bundled her in two blankets and prayed that she would sleep through everything.

Gil had melted snow and stockpiled as much water as he could between the two pots they had.

Susie had collected a diaper and several cloths and a small blanket to wrap the baby in and put them in a neat little pile nearby.

She was lying on her back on Gil's blanket, close to the fire because she was shivering and couldn't seem to get warm.

She was as ready as she could be.

And she was terrified.

But not as terrified as she'd been on the night she'd delivered Carrie, alone in the tiny apartment Roy had rented.

Because this time, she had Gil, who'd been at her side all evening. Distracting her with stories of his childhood exploits. Feeding Carrie the last of one apple that they'd saved all day. Melting pot after pot of snow when she knew he must be tired of crawling through the cave entrance.

Now, he watched her in the flickering firelight while she stared overhead at the rough ceiling.

"I wish there were something I could do for your pain. Are you sure there's not some kind of bark I could use to make a... tea or something?"

She imagined that if they had been in a house not in a cave in the wilderness, he would be standing there wringing his hands. As it was, his concern touched her in a way she hadn't felt in a very long time.

"I'd rather you didn't get lost in the woods trying to look for a willow tree," she said through gritted teeth.

The pain finally passed, and she gulped in a couple of breaths.

"I wouldn't even know what a willow tree looked like," he admitted.

He was such a city slicker. He had indeed

constructed the snare as she'd described to him earlier. He'd admitted that, when he attempted to set it up several dozen yards from the cave, it had become hopelessly tangled.

He carried a revolver, but he'd told her frankly that hitting a small target like a rabbit or squirrel would be almost impossible.

She admired his honesty. He hadn't lied to try to impress her.

But she didn't know what they were going to do if they didn't get rescued soon.

Their meager supply of food had run out.

They'd managed to stretch the small portion of bread and apples as far as they could. As she'd tucked her daughter in for the night, Carrie had whined about being hungry. Susie had soothed her the best she could, but tears had threatened. She'd done her best to hide them.

Susie herself hadn't been hungry all day, not as she'd weathered the labor pains. She was almost certain that Gil hadn't eaten a bite, either, having given Carrie all of the food.

That was admirable, but what would they do come morning?

Gil's thoughts seemed to have traveled the same trail as hers.

"Maybe I should've tried to walk and find a farmhouse," he said.

The driver had claimed there were no farms nearby. But he'd also claimed he would come back for them, and he hadn't.

Another pain came, so intense that she squeezed her eyes closed. "You've been a godsend," she admitted. She didn't want Gil to think she didn't appreciate everything he'd done.

She would never have thought it, not yesterday afternoon when they'd first been stranded together. Gil was surprisingly thoughtful.

Through the spike of pain, she couldn't quiet the niggling voice in her head that wondered when her debt to the man would come due.

Gil was mumbling under his breath. "You need a doctor. Or a midwife. Or anybody other than a bachelor who has no idea what to do."

She couldn't help the strangled cry that emerged from between her teeth.

The pain eased off. "I was all alone when Carrie was born. Even a bachelor is better than that."

"You were? Why?"

She didn't want to admit how things had been with Roy. Not to a man she barely knew. She stared at the wall. "I told you. I've been estranged from my family."

He seemed to accept that answer.

Gil was the only one who actually knew she'd been alone the night of Carrie's birth. Roy hadn't come home that night, hadn't seen his new daughter until the next morning.

Her memories of that night were a hazy blur.

Maybe she should be embarrassed that Gil was witnessing this birth. But she was long past that now.

There was no way to do this privately, not in the small space, not with Gil so close. She would try to retain as much modesty as she could, but from her jumbled memories of Carrie's birth, the pain was only going to get worse. She wanted it to go away. And the only way for that to happen was to have this baby.

"What about your husband?" he asked.

It took a moment for her to trace the thread of conversation her spinning mind had lost. Carrie's birth.

She took one more breath, praying the next pain would wait. She needed another moment of relief.

"My husband was a worse scoundrel than the folks who left us stranded out here."

She hadn't known the depths of his betrayal, hadn't known how deeply she could be hurt until after Carrie was born. He'd promised to change, and she'd stayed. Also, she'd had nowhere to go. She'd been trapped in her marriage with Roy as surely as she was trapped in this cave now.

And in the end, he'd lied. He hadn't given up the

other women. His sins had caught up to him. He'd died a scoundrel's death.

"He left us a long time before he died." Saying the words out loud made her realize the truth in them.

"Why didn't you go back to your family?"

The memory of her last moments with Cecilia—branded into her brain—rose now. The judgement in her sister's expression had sliced her open. Cecilia had been angry, upset.

They both had.

"I can't go back." Shame rolled over her like a creek overflowing its banks, strong enough to drag her under and drown her. "They told me marrying Roy was a bad idea, and I didn't listen."

She barely got the words out before another pain hit.

She didn't realize she had closed her eyes, didn't realize she had reached out until her hands clasped Gil's. His skin was warm and dry, and he allowed the touch. Her eyes flew open, searching. And he was there, close, his gaze filled with concern.

"Sorry," she gasped.

He squeezed her hands once and then loosened his hold. "I can bear it if you can."

He was suddenly blurry. Were those tears in her eyes? She blinked them back.

"I don't suppose your scoundrel of a husband left you any funds to take care of these two babes."

"Of course he didn't." One pain rolled into another. It wasn't letting up. Not much longer now. "I can't think about him right now." She gasped.

The babe shifted inside her, the pressure in her abdomen pooling low.

She let go of Gil. "Help me roll over."

He supported her shoulder as she moved onto her left side. They were truly face to face as she curled into a ball, pulling her knees close to her belly.

"If Carrie wakes up, take her out of here."

He nodded. His eyes were wide and frightened. That was all right.

She was frightened too.

And then the pain just kept going. She couldn't hold back a scream.

GIL KEPT his eyes on Susie's face. He was terrified to look anywhere else.

He wasn't much of a praying man, but he prayed now, that she would be all right and that her baby would be healthy.

Her face and hair were damp with sweat, her face mottled pink.

She was beautiful even in the pain, a terrible kind of beauty. One that showed how strong she was, how resilient, a woman doing what God had made her to do.

He couldn't understand how her husband could have done wrong by her.

Sure, she was a spitfire and stubborn as a cantankerous mule. But that spirit had kept her alive out here. It had reassured her daughter even when Susie must be scared half to death.

She was a good mother. It was obvious in the way that Carrie believed her when she said everything was going to be all right. Carrie had been animated and full of chatter all day, even though he couldn't understand half of what she'd said. Susie knew every garbled word. Carrie was hale and healthy and well-cared for.

What kind of a fool would take the two of them for granted?

These past weeks, as the pain in his lungs had worsened, Gil had lost hope. Lost direction. Even the satisfaction that he usually experienced from playing cards was gone.

But maybe Providence had put him on that stage yesterday. Here was one last good deed he could do before he passed.

Not just taking care of Susie through these difficult hours. What if he could leave her something of himself so she wouldn't be destitute going forward?

Maybe it would even give her a chance to reconcile with her family.

She grabbed onto his hands. Her forehead was furrowed, her teeth gritted. "It's—"

He sensed something change as she exhaled in one big gust of air. She bore down, half-grunting, half-screaming with the effort. She squeezed his hands so hard that her knuckles turned white while his bore the pain.

One breath, and then she was pushing again, screaming again.

Only this time her scream cut off.

She lay there, gasping for breath, panting.

He didn't know what he should do. Was it over? He didn't dare glance at her bare legs on top of the blanket.

She was the one who moved, letting go of him. Reaching down and carefully bringing a squirming, naked body up to hold at her chest.

The baby was red all over, tinier than a loaf of bread. A little mouth opened in a tremulous wail.

Gil snatched one of the blankets from the stack nearby. He dropped it, then fumbled with one of the smaller cloths.

"That's fine," she murmured.

He passed it to her, and she used the cloth to wipe away fluid from the baby's face.

Gil finally found a baby-sized blanket and passed

it to Susie and watched her tuck it around the babe, her movements gentle and familiar.

The terror and pain of a few moments ago seemed completely forgotten as she ran one finger down the baby's forehead and nose. She watched the little one's face like it was the sun rising, tears streaming down her cheeks and a tremulous smile on her lips.

"It's a boy," she whispered.

He couldn't look away from the two of them. This was a true miracle. And he'd been there to witness it.

When she looked up at Gil, joy shone from her eyes. Even in these impossible circumstances, she hadn't lost that.

"Thank you," she whispered.

He swallowed the words of protest that rose to his throat. She shouldn't thank him. He hadn't done anything, not really. He'd kept Carrie company all day and kept the fire going. Right now, he was ready to melt as much snow as she wanted for water to wash.

That wasn't so important.

She was the amazing one.

And he wasn't ready for their time together to be over.

6

The cavalry arrived the next morning before dawn in the form of the stagecoach driver, a sheriff, and two other men from town. The foursome had ridden up in two horse-drawn sleighs.

Susie had never been happier to see a group of strangers. The driver was shocked to find her holding Albert, swaddled tightly in a blanket for warmth. Over the past forty-eight hours, she'd imagined railing at him for leaving her and Carrie and Gil stranded. But he apologized profusely, and in her exhaustion, she was content to allow Gil to give him a dressing down. Which he did, and in much harsher terms than Susie would have used.

The men had brought food, and Carrie had stuffed herself until she was full and drowsy. Gil was ushered onto one sled, while Susie and her two children were bundled onto the other.

Susie tucked a blanket around Carrie, who was practically glued to her side. The girl had been woken abruptly to find a baby brother, a group of strangers, and her mama rushing her out of the cave. If she was a little clingy, it was allowed.

Susie lifted her gaze to meet Gil's from where he sat in the sleigh several feet away. Even from here, his blue eyes were striking. She hadn't seen him in full light since the first afternoon when they'd been stranded. She'd known objectively that he was handsome, but sometime over the past hours, his kindness and thoughtfulness had blurred his good looks somehow. Or maybe his handsomeness had become less important during her desperation and pain.

Now, in the bright morning light, with some distance between them, she saw him as if for the first time.

His suit was wrinkled, and he had a smudge of soot on one cheek. His jaw hadn't seen a razor in days, and golden stubble only served to highlight his ruggedness. His eyes were piercing, and her stomach suddenly plummeted.

He didn't look away, but the sheriff driving the second sleigh urged it forward. The motion broke the connection between them, and Susie dropped her gaze to her lap. What was that?

Her face was hot, and her pulse rushed between her ears. The sensations were familiar and unwelcome. She'd felt the same shock of attraction with Roy in the beginning. And look where she'd ended up.

After a quick stop at the stagecoach to collect the luggage, they were on their way. Hannah was expecting them. But Susie was too tired and uncertain to be excited about finally seeing her friend again. Carrie dozed off and on, but Susie fretted over the unwanted attraction to Gil Hart until the sleighs arrived in town just before lunch.

All four of them, Gil included, had been taken to the doctor's office. Gil had refused to see the man, walking away on his own steam. The doctor had briefly checked over Susie, Carrie, and Albert, pronouncing them all in excellent health after their adventure.

Hannah met them on the boardwalk. By that time, Albert was crying and hungry and Carrie was wide awake and ready for adventure. Susie just wanted a place to hide.

Hannah embraced her tightly. "I'm so glad you're all right. When I heard they left you…" Anger hummed in her words, but she didn't finish the sentence.

Susie understood, though. "I'm just glad we finally made it."

Hannah took them upstairs to her apartment over a milliner's store and shooed Susie into the tiny bedroom. She told her to rest for as long as she needed. And after the baby had been fed and changed, Susie fell into a dreamless sleep, one that was only broken when Albert woke to eat.

During one of the middle-of-the-night feedings, Susie told herself that she would be ready to start making plans in the morning. She hadn't thought past surviving the cold. Before that, she had only thought of reaching Hannah and starting over.

It was time to figure out what she was going to do.

Only when early morning light was filtering through the window in the tiny kitchen did she register Hannah's tension. Susie sat at the tiny round table and watched her friend scramble an egg on the stove.

In the bedroom, Albert was tucked in a borrowed cradle, and Carrie was sleeping on a pallet on the floor at the end of the bed. She could sleep through anything and hadn't woken once during the night when Albert had cried.

Hannah had.

The apartment was so small that there was only the one bed. Hannah had been generous enough to share. Susie had tried her best to be quiet, not to rock when she'd risen to take care of Albert. But Hannah had woken every time.

Hannah had never been married. They'd met in Silver Springs when Roy had spent several weeks there, gambling away the money he'd won at their last stop. When Roy and Susie had moved on, her friendship with Hannah had continued through occasional letters. After Roy died, she'd offered Susie a place to stay as long as she needed it.

But it seemed something had changed.

Hannah wasn't smiling this morning, and Susie worried that she was already trying to figure out how to ask Susie to leave.

Living with a brand new baby wasn't easy. And Susie hadn't expected the apartment to be so small.

"It won't be like that every night," she said.

Hannah glanced over her shoulder.

"He'll start sleeping for longer stretches," Susie explained. She didn't say that it might take weeks for that to happen.

"It's fine." But Hannah's voice didn't sound fine.

Just then, Albert wailed.

And Carrie appeared in the bedroom doorway. "Albert's crying," she said. "He cries a lot."

Susie felt a little like crying herself. She forgotten how great the exhaustion was in these early days, only being able to snatch a few hours of sleep between feedings. Albert was a voracious eater.

Susie was worried that those hours spent in the cave before he'd been born, when there hadn't been enough food to go around, had hurt him somehow. But Albert seemed content and healthy.

Susie settled Carrie in the chair she had occupied at the table and broke her toast into smaller pieces, moving quickly.

"Stay in your chair," she told her daughter. "If you're still hungry, I'll scramble you an egg when I'm done feeding Albert."

She retreated to the bedroom and loosened the top buttons of her dress, preparing to nurse the baby. When she picked him up from the cradle, his fussing quieted.

She sat on the edge of the bed and held him close. In moments like these, she couldn't look away from his face, already so dear to her. He latched on hungrily, and his small fist clenched around her finger when she reached to gently touch his cheek.

What was she going to do?

Hannah said everything was fine now, but her patience would eventually run out.

Roy's had.

When Carrie had been an infant, the sleepless nights had worn him out. He had stayed several nights in a hotel rather than coming home. She hadn't guessed then, but he hadn't spent those nights alone. Would things have been different for them if

Carrie hadn't been born? Would Susie have chased him if she hadn't been pregnant? Or would she have let him go, ashamed of the liberties she'd let him take but with no one the wiser to her secret?

She didn't know.

And thinking about *what ifs* didn't change anything.

She loved her daughter more than life itself. She wouldn't change a thing. Well, maybe she would change Roy's attitude toward marriage and fatherhood.

She'd thought coming to stay with Hannah would open up more options for her. But what kind of job would there be for her in a town this small? More laundry, more mending?

She knew the tears that threatened were more a result of the ordeal she'd survived than her current circumstances. The cave, sleepless nights, giving birth.

The emotion would pass. And she would get through this. She had to.

She had fed, burped, and changed Albert when Hannah slipped into the room, closing the door behind her. Her friend's eyes showed more life than they had earlier.

"You've got a gentleman caller."

What? Susie was confused at first, but Hannah's meaning became clear when she straightened the collar of Susie's dress. It must've gotten tucked inside when she had put herself back together.

Hannah waggled her eyebrows. "He's a handsome one. Sharp dresser."

Gil. It had to be.

Susie felt her face flush as she stood. She couldn't very well ask Hannah to send him away, not when he had kept her and Carrie from starving and helped her through Albert's birth.

But neither could she forget those last moments as they'd bundled into the sleds.

Dread twisted her stomach into a knot. Roy had taught her that nothing in life came for free. No doubt Gil was here to collect on the debt she had amassed for herself by leaning on him during the past few days.

She'd known it was coming, and yet somehow his kindness there at the very end, the softness she'd imagined she'd seen in his eyes… She had begun to hope that she was wrong about him.

There was nothing to do now but face it.

Hannah sent her a wary glance. "Let me take the baby."

Hannah hadn't held the baby once and had seemed almost afraid of him the past hours. Susie didn't know why, but she also saw no reason to force him on her friend right now.

"I'm all right."

She opened the bedroom door to see Gil sitting on the sofa. Carrie was standing at his knee, chattering, and Susie experienced a fuzzy memory of him spinning a tall tale about a bunny rabbit.

He looked up, and his eyes weren't soft at all. He wore a determined look that made her heart drop to her toes.

GIL'S LUNGS were burning this morning, though he'd barely been outside. Only to walk down the boardwalk from the hotel to see Susie. Maybe he should've stayed in bed longer.

But he couldn't wait to put his plan in motion.

He had felt a thrill the night Albert had been born. He could pinpoint the exact moment that Susie had looked into his eyes and something had connected deep inside him.

He likened that connection to the feeling he got when he was in the middle of a poker hand and *knew* the next card that would be played. From that point on, everything unfolded in the hand exactly the way it should.

He'd had the Midas touch last night in the local saloon. After he'd strode away from the doctor's office, he'd checked into the hotel down the street. He'd bathed and shaved, napped for a short time, and hit the tables. But after he'd won a half-dozen hands and lost zero, a restless feeling had him excusing himself much earlier than he usually turned in. He'd gone to sleep thinking of Susie and the plans that were unfolding before him like a royal flush—a perfect hand.

He was certain of his course. Being with Susie was a sure bet.

So when she emerged from the only other room in this tiny apartment with her expression full of trepidation, he was surprised.

Carrie tapped on his knee, and he realized he had lost the thread of conversation.

"I named my new dolly Gil. Just like you."

He was charmed by the statement and couldn't help smiling, even as he hoped she hadn't really named her blond-haired, blue-eyed doll after him. Surely not.

The girl cradled the porcelain doll in her arms and smoothed the hair on its head.

Susie crossed the floor quickly, putting a hand on Carrie's shoulder. "What is that? Where did you get it?"

"I gave it to her," he said easily. "I thought she deserved something nice after... after everything."

He'd seen the doll in a shop window on his way over here. It had made him think of Carrie, and he'd wanted to purchase it for her. So he had.

But Susie looked dismayed. "Carrie—"

The woman, Susie's friend, who had answered the door and let him in, now moved forward to crowd around Carrie as well. "Miss Carrie, why don't we take a walk and let your mama have a moment with Mr. Hart?"

Susie started to protest, but her friend gave her a wide-eyed look that communicated something beyond Gil's grasp. Susie relinquished her hold on Carrie, but not before she'd swiftly removed the doll from her arms. It was quite a feat, considering she held baby Albert to one shoulder.

The woman and girl were out of the apartment in a blink, which left Gil alone with Susie. Finally.

She extended the doll toward him. "It's a kind gesture, but we can't accept it."

He frowned. "It's not a gesture. It's a gift."

"It's too expensive."

Too expensive. The money didn't matter to him. He couldn't take it with him. "She seemed to like it."

"She did like it, but we can't accept it." She set the doll on the sofa beside him.

Why was she arguing with him? Didn't she want Carrie to have something nice? Based on everything he knew about her, she'd give her daughter the clothes off her back if Carrie needed them.

Her lips were set in a stubborn line he'd already

begun to recognize. "All gifts have strings. I owe you too much already."

Gifts had strings? What was she talking about? "This one doesn't."

She made a noise that was somewhere between a growl and a shriek, though at a low volume as she bounced Albert in her arms. She turned and stalked away, but there was nowhere for her to go in the tiny space.

They were getting off track. He hadn't come here to argue about the doll. He hadn't come here to argue at all.

"Would you sit down for a minute? There's something I want to talk to you about."

She whirled, her mouth open as if she meant to tell him off, though he couldn't imagine what she would say. Hadn't they parted on good terms outside the cave? He hadn't hung around the doctor's office —couldn't stand being examined. Maybe she was angry that he hadn't said good-bye?

She snapped her teeth closed with an audible click and blanked the expression from her face. She moved slowly to the chair across from where he sat and perched on the very edge, almost as if she were prepared to run away. She looked braced for the worst.

He cleared his throat. "I think we should get married."

Her jaw dropped open, and her cheeks pinked with color. She drew back and shook her head.

He hadn't meant to blurt it out like that. He tried again. "Hear me out. This consumption is going to-to kill me." His voice broke, and he inhaled a fiery breath. It wasn't only his lungs that burned. He didn't want to think about the end and how it would come. But there wasn't much time left. "I thought... Well, you've got two little ones to take care of and no money. Unless I'm wrong. If so, tell me now."

She shook her head slowly. "You aren't wrong."

"I've got plenty of money, and I want to leave it to you. I think we should get married and in a few weeks or months, when my time is up, you inherit everything."

She lurched out of the chair and crossed to the small window in the kitchen. She peered out of it. What was she looking for?

"I think maybe you should see the doctor," she said. She didn't look at him.

Huh?

She glanced at him. "Perhaps you need a doctor for your brain. You sound crazy."

He let out a huff. "I've had enough of doctors. I've seen several, and they all tell me the same thing. And maybe I've just had longer to think about this than you have. It's a good idea."

She shook her head. "It's outlandish."

The baby stirred, and she settled him on her shoulder with a rub to his back. He snuggled into her neck, perfectly content in his mother's arms.

He gestured to the room around them. "How long are you going to be happy staying here?"

A shadow passed behind her eyes. Surely things weren't already difficult with her friend.

"I've got plenty of money for you to buy a house. You and the children would have everything you need. You wouldn't want for anything."

Her eyes narrowed, and she blinked a couple of times. Maybe she was thinking about it. She bit her lip. "I don't want to get married again. My husband... my marriage was not good."

"This wouldn't be like that. You don't love me. I don't love you."

She flinched, and he regretted the harshness of his words. Surely by now she knew he didn't always say the right thing. He tried again, "I mean, we like each other well enough. We got along fine when we were trapped in that cave."

"Because we didn't have another choice." Her voice was high, near panic.

He didn't want to upset her. Couldn't she see this was the perfect plan? He wouldn't have to be alone for his last days. He hadn't realized how much it mattered until now. And she'd be left with all his earthly possessions. He was good at counting cards.

He rarely lost. And he had a nice bank account to show for it.

This would work, if only she'd trust him.

"If you find out you don't like me any better than your first husband, you're only stuck with me for a short time."

She pressed her free hand to her forehead. He hadn't thought this would be a difficult decision. It made perfect sense. Maybe he just wasn't explaining it in the right way.

"When we were in that cave, you said you'd do anything for Carrie. Why not spend a few weeks with me? Why not give your children a better life?"

7

"I don't understand why you won't consider him."

Susie glared at Hannah. Partly because this wasn't any of her nosy friend's business. And partly because there was a small corner of her mind that agreed with Hannah. A very small corner. A minuscule corner.

She'd had one day to think about Gil's outlandish proposal. Another day in the tiny apartment where every noise seemed magnified. Another night of holding her breath and praying she didn't bump into anything and wake Hannah every time Albert needed to eat. Another night when Hannah had woken every time.

Now it was late afternoon. Carrie had gotten up from her nap not long before and was playing with her new porcelain doll, because Gil had refused her refusal of his gift. Carrie was pretending to be a little mother, taking the baby into the bedroom to lay it in Albert's cradle. Her pretend baby would wake up and require her to change it and rock it and sing to it. And then the whole thing would start all over again.

Susie was thankful her daughter was distracted, because she didn't want Carrie to overhear what Hannah was saying. The girl was already too attached to Gil.

Everything had happened too quickly. They'd been trapped in the cave and spent hours upon hours together. If that stage wheel had never broken, she might never have spoken to Gil.

This consumption is going to kill me.

Gil's words had shaken her. She knew life was precious and bodies were fragile, but Gil wasn't that much older than she was. It frightened her to think that he could be gone in such a short time.

"I don't see what your dilemma is," Hannah said.

"I promised myself I was never going to marry again."

"So what? I lie to myself and say I won't have a second piece of pie. We all do it. All the time."

"I wasn't lying to myself. I've told you some of what passed between Roy and me." She'd been far too ashamed to share the darkest parts of her marriage with anyone else.

Why hadn't she been enough for Roy? Was she so boring, with her small-town roots, that she couldn't hold his interest? Why had he turned to other women?

Was she that unlovable?

She'd told Hannah the least of it. That Roy had been difficult and raised his voice when he was angry.

But there was so much more. "I felt like... like a wild animal caught in a trapper's snare. I don't ever want to experience that again."

"But if you *are* trapped, it's only for a short time."

Gil had said as much when he'd told her the marriage wouldn't last long. "Unless he's lying," she said.

She didn't want to think it. Death was a very serious thing to lie about. What if Gil had made the whole thing up? What if it wasn't consumption he suffered but only a bad cold?

What if he'd get better and live a long, long life?

Would a man lie about something like that?

She hadn't imagined Roy could lie to her face, but he had, often.

She was too trusting. She wasn't good at discerning truth from lie.

She glanced through the doorway to see Carrie standing in the bedroom, rocking her baby. She was humming and content.

"What about Carrie? What happens when she has a father figure in her life one day and the next he's gone?"

Carrie had already lost Roy. She had been several months shy of two when he'd passed away, and Susie had been mired in grief, pregnant, confused, and alone. And broke.

She hadn't known what to tell Carrie when she'd asked for her father. After a while, Carrie had stopped asking.

"Do you remember anything from when you were that young?"

Susie shrugged. She couldn't say exactly.

Hannah seemed to want to play devil's advocate, arguing with every reason Susie had for refusing Gil's unconventional proposal.

It was crazy to even consider going through with it.

So why hadn't she said no outright?

Why not give your children a better life?

The man had known exactly the words to say. Words that had kept her up all night, even after Albert had been fed and soothed back to sleep.

She loved Carrie and Albert. So much that she would do anything for them. Apparently, that included considering marrying a man she barely knew purely for his money.

"You should at least meet him for dinner," Hannah said.

Before he'd left, Gil had asked her to come for dinner at the hotel so they could discuss the matter further.

Susie hadn't decided yet whether she would go. Wouldn't it make him angry if she accepted his dinner invitation but not his offer of marriage?

What if he talked her into it?

She was still vacillating when, that evening, she climbed the boardwalk steps to the hotel.

She stared at the door, memories surfacing. She had first met Roy in a hotel dining room. She'd contrived the meeting, pretended to be there to meet a friend who hadn't shown up. She'd caught Roy's interest. They'd talked. And look at everything that had happened after that.

No good could come of this.

Yet... She took a deep breath and went inside.

But Gil was not waiting in the lobby, as he had promised. She nodded to the desk clerk and waited near the door.

This hotel was notably smaller than the one in Bear Creek. It might've once been a two-story house. A staircase with a banister took up one wall of the lobby area. Behind the clerk's desk, the dining room looked remarkably like her mother's sitting room.

She couldn't help but wonder how many rooms there were available to rent out. Three? Maybe four?

When Gil still hadn't appeared after several minutes, she approached the desk.

"I was supposed to meet Mr. Hart at five. Do you know if he's come down yet?"

"I haven't seen Mr. Hart today." The clerk seemed very young, as if he hadn't yet hit the years when he would be able to grow a mustache or beard. He also seemed hesitant, as if he didn't quite know what to do with her.

Maybe Gil had left town, taking his proposal with him.

But Susie knew she wouldn't truly rest until the matter was settled.

"Would you mind knocking on his door?"

The young man looked uncertain, and she smiled kindly at him. Her smiles had always won favor in the past, and apparently, despite the hard years she'd lived, it still had an effect on the opposite sex.

He nodded and crossed behind her to ascend the staircase. She could see the upstairs hallway through the banister rail.

She glanced down at herself self-consciously. She remembered the post-pregnancy belly from after Carrie had been born, and this one was no different. If anything, worse. She disliked the way she looked right now. Flabby and exhausted. She couldn't fit into her regular dresses yet, so she'd been forced to wear this one, which looked like a tent. She had wrapped a dark shawl around her shoulders and hoped that the folded ends of it would hide her awful middle.

Perhaps it was wrong of her to care so much about her looks. She wasn't vain. At least she didn't think so, no matter how many times her sister Cecilia had teased her in the past.

Was it a sin to want to look one's best? She didn't think so.

She heard the murmur of the clerk's voice. Gil must have a room near the front of the hotel. She couldn't hear what he said, but an awful cough rang out, reaching her ears. It seemed loud enough to rattle the windows.

She heard the door close with a soft snick. Gil hadn't stopped coughing by the time the clerk reached the bottom of the stairs.

"Mr. Hart was indisposed. He asked me to tell you that he would call on you another time."

Gil was still coughing.

"Is he ill? Does he need help?"

The clerk held his hands in front of his body, his expression both wary and worried. "It isn't my place to say. I'm supposed to run the front desk, help guests if they need fresh linens…"

He was young, so she forgave him for not taking more interest in the problem.

"If you don't mind, I'll just check on him myself."

The clerk made a noise of protest, but she ignored him and lifted her skirts and hurried up the stairs. She stopped outside the first door on the left, where she had seen the clerk's legs through the banister.

Gil had gone quiet, but she couldn't forget that racking cough.

She remembered another hotel doorway. A snowy morning when she had snuck away from the family ranch and stood outside Roy's doorway. She hadn't cared whether it was right or wrong. She'd believed she loved him and had wanted to be with him no matter what.

She'd been so easily led astray. She was a fool.

This was different. At least that's what she told herself.

Her hand was shaking as she raised it. She fought through the panic that her memories unleashed and gave one sharp knock before she pushed open the door.

The curtains had been opened, and there was still enough light outside that she could see where Gil lay in the bed. The covers were mussed, as if he'd thrown them off at some time.

It was the man who arrested her attention. His

cheeks were flushed, his eyes unfocused and glassy. It took him far too long to focus on her.

When he registered that it was Susie standing in the doorway, he rose up on his elbow. "What are you—?"

His words were lost in a coughing fit, each harsh one rattling out of his chest. She could see how he struggled for breath as his shoulders heaved.

There was a pitcher of water on the dresser, but the glass at his bedside table was empty. Had the clerk even thought to fill it?

This was different from the time she had spent with Roy. Seeing Gil sick made the decision for her.

She stepped over the threshold, though she left the door open for propriety's sake.

Gil was trying to say something. He coughed, rasped out a quick "Go"—another cough—"away." Several more coughs followed, until spittle was flying from his mouth, and he was wheezing.

She fetched the water pitcher.

She wasn't going away.

Not when she'd found the way to erase her debt.

THE LAST THING on earth Gil wanted Susie to witness was him lost to a coughing fit that was so bad that he couldn't catch his breath.

But she ignored his protest—more of a grunt and gesture toward the door—and brought him a glass of water. The only reason he took it was because his throat felt like it was on fire.

She waited until he had emptied the glass and then refilled it.

He hadn't realized he was this thirsty, and he was grateful for the drink. Now, if she would just leave.

She didn't. She scowled at him. "You should've sent a note that you were ill. I would've come sooner."

He shook his head. His throat felt wrong, but at least he wasn't coughing. For the moment. "I'd rather you didn't see me like this."

"So you've changed your mind about getting married?"

He shook his head, wary.

"Because a wife would care for you, all the way until the end."

He hadn't given any thought to that. He'd only thought of providing for her. Maybe it was too late anyway. Every breath felt like flames of fire.

"There's nothing to be ashamed of," she said. "You saw me at my worst."

"There was no worst," he rasped. "You were fierce and beautiful."

She looked at him with an expression both surprised and uncertain.

In the cave, she'd been frightened and resigned and determined to bring her baby into the world. Through it all, she'd been amazing.

This was different. He'd spiked a fever during the night and had sweated through his nightshirt, though now he was shivering. His hair was matted with sweat and he was fighting for every breath.

"Please let me fetch the doctor."

He shook his head so violently that it set off another bout of coughing. This one didn't last quite as long, but she had to help prop him up to a sitting position to get it to subside.

When he could, he swallowed. "I've seen all the doctors I intend to see. They all say the same thing. There's nothing that can be done. I've had a fever like this before." Though his coughing had never been quite so bad. "It took two days but the fever subsided. Either it will go the same way, or..." He would expire.

Her expression became tinged with sadness, and he was relieved to know that she did care. That boded well for his marriage plan. As long as his body could make it through this setback.

"Have you eaten today?"

He only gave a tiny shake of his head this time.

"I'm going to make sure Carrie is settled for the night and check on Albert. Then I'll find you some broth."

"You must still be exhausted." She'd mentioned yesterday that there wasn't much sleep to be had with a new baby around. "You don't have to do all that. Tell the clerk to send up some soup, and I will make it worth his while."

She propped one hand on her hip. "After everything that happened in that cave, do you really think I'm going to just leave you here like this?" Her chin was set at a determined angle. "This will settle the debt between us."

It wasn't the first time she mentioned debt. He sorely needed to disabuse her of that notion. There was no debt between them.

But another coughing fit took him, and this time she couldn't hide her worry.

She was gone moments later with a promise to return.

8

G il's fever spiked.

In his delirium, he saw his mother sitting at his bedside.

A damp cloth was laid on his forehead, and its coolness was both a shock and a relief.

He drifted.

The next time he woke, he was lucid. Susie was there, in his room. She sat on the bed, with her back to him.

If this was the end, he wanted to see her face.

He tried to speak her name, but only a rattling breath emerged. She glanced over her shoulder and registered that he was awake. She didn't turn to face him like he expected. He couldn't see what she was doing, but her small, jerky movements wiggled the bed slightly.

When she stood and turned, she was holding Albert high on her shoulder, patting his back more forcefully than Gil would've expected. Burping the baby, he realized.

Which meant he'd just interrupted a feeding. She was caring for the both of them at the same time.

She rocked slightly from side to side. "I'm sorry, I…" Her cheeks were rosy with a blush.

He tried to tell her that it was all right. He hadn't seen anything he shouldn't.

But his voice still wasn't working right.

She moved across the room and gently laid the baby in a cradle she must've convinced the hotel clerk to deliver.

And then she was back at Gil's bedside, helping him sit up. Holding a glass of water to his lips when his hand shook too much to support it.

After he'd drank half the glass, he let his head fall back, though he stayed propped on his elbow. He felt as weak as a newborn kitten.

And scared.

He couldn't seem to draw a full breath.

"Where's Carrie?" he rasped.

Her brows drew together in a look that expressed her surprise and curiosity. "She's sleeping over at Hannah's place. Hannah is watching her."

Good. That was good.

She lifted a bowl and spoon from the bedside

table. "This is cold now, but you should eat something if you feel up to it."

He didn't much want to, but he let her ply him with spoonfuls of chilled broth.

Albert made a peep from his cradle, and Susie looked in that direction, but the baby didn't cry.

She raised another spoonful of broth to Gil's lips. "He was crying to wake the dead only a few minutes ago. Is that what woke you?"

He shook his head slightly. "Didn't hear him at all," he whispered.

"If he wakes the other tenants, we might be asked to leave."

She was worried. If he had breath, he would tell her that the clerk had told him yesterday he was the hotel's only customer.

He liked that she was worrying about staying here with him.

He waved off the spoon when he couldn't take another bite. She put the bowl back on the bedside table, and he registered the tiny lines fanning around her eyes and mouth.

She must be exhausted, staying up to take care of him while she was also caring for a newborn.

She was something.

He wished he'd met her sooner.

She sat on the edge of the bed again and touched his forehead with the back of her wrist.

"Your fever worries me. Won't you let me fetch the doctor?"

"No more doctors," he whispered. He'd been poked and prodded and filled to the brim with medicines at a Colorado sanatorium. He'd been told he was one of the cases they couldn't cure. He'd sought a second and third opinion, certain that his money could buy him a better answer.

Turned out, it couldn't.

"Then I suppose you should rest." Her fingers brushed through the hair at his temple, soothing him.

His eyes began to flutter closed, but the weight on his chest was terrifying. What if he fell asleep and never woke up? His eyes flew open.

"Tell me," he whispered, "why won't you go home? Is your family that terrible?"

She frowned, but when it was clear he wasn't going back to sleep, she said, "The mother who gave birth to me died when I was about eight. There are three of us sisters. One older and one younger. Velma was only a few months old when our mother passed, and Cecilia and I raised her ourselves because our stepfather was a no-account drunk." She still sounded bitter, after all those years. "He died about a year later."

So Susie and her sisters had been all alone in the world? His heart ached for her.

He made a noise that was meant to be comforting, but maybe she thought he was in pain because she patted his hand.

"We had a schoolteacher who was a mite too curious. Sarah saw how our stepfather neglected us, and she tried to help us. She ended up getting herself fired by the school board for it." Her eyes were far-off, and she shook her head. He wanted to know more of that story, but she was already going on.

"She met Oscar about the same time. He was a horse trainer, traveling through town. He—" She glanced at him and there was a softness in her eyes. "He made her an outlandish offer. He would marry her so she could take care of me and my sisters. They adopted us."

An outlandish offer. It was no coincidence that she'd used the same words to talk about her father that she'd used when she'd tried to talk herself out of Gil's proposal. It was obvious from the gentle tone in her voice that these were good memories.

He was going to win her over. As long as he didn't die tonight.

She was still talking, but his eyes grew heavy, and sleep finally overtook him.

He woke coughing. She turned up the lamp at his bedside and helped prop him up as his chest heaved. He knew his eyes must look a little wild because she seemed pale and frightened. It felt like a horse—or maybe the broken stagecoach—was sitting on his chest.

When his coughing finally ceased, he dragged in breath after breath, but none of them satisfied his need for air.

She gave him more water to drink.

"Tell me more about your family," he whispered.

She touched his temple, his cheek, his ear. "Your fever's so high that you won't remember in the morning."

"I'll remember. Please."

She settled on the bed beside him.

"Oscar, my adopted father, was orphaned when he was a boy. His father Jonas adopted him and six other boys. And one little girl. All of that before he met my grandmother, Penny."

That must have been a wild house to grow up in. All those boys, all under a bachelor's care.

"They were a rough and tumble bunch until they started getting married. Mama was the first one to marry into the family. She's very proper." A schoolteacher? He could see that. Had Susie always felt like she couldn't measure up?

"Tell me about... your sisters."

"Velma's as sweet as apple pie, smart as a whip. She's... fifteen now." She sounded surprised to realize it.

"And your other sister?"

Where Susie's eyes had been soft and full of fond memories when she'd spoken of her younger sister, now a hard light entered them. "Cecilia followed in Mama's footsteps. She became a schoolteacher. She's always had her own idea of how everyone around her should act. Prim and proper. Always doing what they're supposed to. Never getting out of line."

Was she talking about the children in this Cecilia's classroom? Or was she talking about herself? Based on the bitterness that laced every word, it was the latter.

"Maybe she's changed since you've seen her last. How long has it been?"

Susie looked down at the bedspread, shaking her head. "It's been three years. And I don't think Cecilia will ever change. She's very certain of who she is."

"I bet you've changed though." When her gaze snapped to his, he went on. "You're unselfish. You look after your children. You didn't eat a thing that day in the cave so that Carrie would have enough food."

Maybe she blushed a little. He couldn't tell in the dim light. "Any mother would've done that."

A thin wail came from Albert's crib, and she stood up. She seemed almost relieved to cross to the crib. "You'd better rest some more. It won't do if he wakes the entire hotel."

He meant to argue, but his eyes slid closed again.

He didn't wake up.

He only knew that the pressure on his chest had grown worse.

Every breath was a gasp.

He couldn't seem to open his eyes.

Susie was still there. He felt her touch his cheek. Sensed she was saying something, though he couldn't hear her words.

Was this the end?

SUSIE STARED at the telephone tucked against the wall in one corner of the general store.

She had already been here for too long, staring at the machine for several minutes, trying to gather the courage to dial home. She held Albert in her arms. After a long, sleepless night, he seemed heavier than usual. He was also restless. She knew he would need to eat soon.

Maybe she should return to Gil.

His last coughing fit had frightened her. He had gasped for breath, and for a terrifying few moments, she had worried he would suffocate.

How many times had he refused to see the doctor? Too many.

Did he want to die?

She couldn't imagine that the man who had

fought so hard to keep them alive in that cave would just give up.

There was only one thing she could think to do.

And it happened to be the very last thing she wanted to do.

Gil's questions about her family had made her ponder everything she had missed for the past three years.

And thinking about all her uncles had brought on memories of Maxwell and his wife Hattie, both doctors back in Bear Creek.

Surely phoning a member of her family who happened to be a doctor wasn't the same as bringing a doctor to Gil's hotel room.

Or maybe she just wanted an excuse to phone home. Maxwell was always compassionate. He'd bandaged her knee when she'd fallen from a horse at ten years old. He'd always listened when she'd talked about her struggles in school.

He could help Gil. Couldn't he?

There was nothing for it.

She shifted Albert to one arm and picked up the handset. She raised it to her ear and asked the operator to connect her to Uncle Maxwell in Bear Creek.

It was her uncle who answered.

"Uncle Maxwell?"

"Cecilia?" Hearing her sister's name brought a

rush of homesickness. So Cecilia didn't live in Bear Creek?

Susie pushed away the questions. "No, it's me. Susie."

She heard his audible gasp.

"We've been praying for you. Worrying about you. Are you all right? Where are you? Are you coming home?" It was a shock to hear his caring questions. She'd thought they must hate her for how she'd left.

She couldn't think about home. Couldn't bear it, not when Gil needed her.

She took a shaky breath. "I'm not coming home. But I do need your help."

There was a pause, and she wondered if he was angry at her answer. Maybe he would hang up. She didn't deserve anything else.

But the line stayed connected. "What can I do?"

"There's someone special…" She didn't know how to describe Gil. They were barely friends. "He has consumption, and he's been having these coughing attacks. They've gotten worse and worse, and now he can barely breathe. I have to do something."

Maybe it was because Gil had taken care of her through Albert's birth. She said that her caring for his cough would fulfill the debt she owed him, but it was more than that.

She didn't want to lose him.

Maxwell's voice was muffled on the other end of the line. Was he talking to Hattie? If he was trying to somehow find out where Susie was and come after her, she would hang up. But she held the line, hoping and praying that he would be able to help Gil.

"Without examining this man myself, I can't say for sure. Hattie's had some success in relieving a bad cough with a poultice made of crushed garlic bulbs." He explained the process of making the poultice.

He finished with, "I don't know how effective it will be."

At least this gave her some direction. Something to take action on.

Albert roused and began nuzzling her collarbone. She knew it would only be a few moments before he was screaming his hunger for everyone to hear.

Her time was up.

Her eyes smarted, and she didn't know if it was from hearing a dear voice from her past or the fact that Maxwell had tried to help her.

"Thank you," she whispered.

"Susie, we want you to come home. Even if it's just for a visit. Your mama—"

"Don't tell her I called," she said quickly.

It wasn't fair to ask it. She didn't even know why it mattered.

There wasn't anything Sarah could do from Bear Creek. She hadn't revealed her location.

"I-I have to go."

Albert began to cry in earnest, and she hung up the telephone. After a deep breath designed to put her emotions back where they belonged, she went to find the shopkeeper. She needed as much garlic as she could find.

GIL ROUSED A FEW TIMES, never opening his eyes.

What was that awful smell? It burned his nostrils.

Or maybe that was sulfur, and this was hell.

No. Someone—he thought it must be Susie—nursed him with water and light broth.

How much time had passed? He didn't know. Maybe hours, maybe days.

Gradually, the flames in his lungs began to flicker and then die.

When he finally opened his eyes, he caught sight of Susie sleeping in the chair. Her cheek was pillowed on her folded hands, her knees drawn up so that her feet were off the floor.

Her hair was falling out of its pins, and her cheeks were flushed with sleep. She was a sight to wake up to. He only moved his eyes, afraid that if he shifted his body, it would bring back the fire in his lungs.

Albert was sleeping peacefully in his cradle.

Gil must've made some noise, or maybe she was used to waking up at the tiniest sound because of the baby. She opened her eyes, and they landed unerringly on him.

"You're awake," she said. "How do you feel?"

He pushed himself to a seated position. Remarkably, that didn't set him coughing. "Better. I feel better. What did you do?"

"We can talk about that later. Do you feel up to eating?"

His stomach was actually growling, but he was more aware of the stench of sickly sweat than anything else. That and the fact that he badly needed a shave. "How long…?"

Shadows passed behind her eyes. "Three days. Things got worse before they got better."

"Thank you. For staying."

Their gazes connected. He had more to say, but that stench wasn't going away.

"I'll be up for something to eat as soon as I have a bath," he said. "Could you have some hot water sent up?"

She nodded. The baby began to make a wuffling noise, and she rose, stretching out a kink in her back.

"And then I think we have some business to take care of."

She glanced at him, eyes narrowed. She must've heard the serious tone in his voice.

These past days had shown him just how short his time was. One more episode like this, and he wouldn't survive. He could feel it.

He wanted things settled before that happened.

"I think we can consider it taken care of," she said.

His heart lurched. After everything, was she going to turn him down?

"I had plenty of time to think. And you're right. I will marry you. For Carrie and for Albert."

She glanced at the window and squinted. She was holding something back. He wasn't surprised when she spoke again. "However, I need you to make me a promise."

He couldn't imagine what it would be. But he nodded. Anything to get her to accept.

"You have to promise you won't fall in love with me. It-it would only complicate things between us."

Her words brought on an immediate urge to chuckle, but she looked so serious that he swallowed it back. Was this really something to be worried about? He had only weeks to live.

He didn't see how it mattered, so he nodded. "I promise I won't fall in love with you."

He pointed to the satchel on top of the dresser. "Can you bring that to me?"

She fetched it and handed it to him. From inside, he drew out a small leather pouch. He pulled out the ring from inside.

It was a gold band with a simple pearl.

She'd been watching curiously, but now she started to draw away.

He caught her hand in his.

Maybe he was smelly and ought to wait, but he wasn't giving her a chance to back out.

"You've already agreed," he reminded her. "This belonged to my grandmother." The ring was one of the only things he had taken when he'd left home. The break with his father had been painful, with tempers lost and shouting on both sides. But his mother had slipped this to him while he was packing his things.

Susie allowed him to slip it onto the third finger of her left hand. She stared down at it for a moment, blinking rapidly.

"I'm glad you said yes."

But she swallowed and nodded and gently extracted her hand from his. "I'll wait for you to call. I'll be at Hannah's."

And then she was gone.

9

Susie couldn't help the way her hands trembled as she clutched the single poinsettia that Hannah had scrounged up from who knew where.

She had agreed to marry Gil one week ago, and the day was here.

This was her last chance to change her mind.

Hannah was sitting on a straight-backed wooden bench in the back of the local barbershop, Albert in her arms. It turned out that the barber was also a preacher and was going to be the one who married Susie and Gil today. Carrie sat on the bench next to Hannah, her legs swinging back and forth. As usual, she was chattering nonstop to poor Hannah, who seemed to be struggling to follow the toddler's flow of conversation.

Susie couldn't hear what she said, but that might be due to the rushing in her ears.

What if this was a mistake?

Gil stood near the front window of the barbershop. The barber had locked up for a short time so no unexpected customers would interrupt them. Her husband-to-be wore a new, dark brown suit. He'd claimed the suit he'd worn when they had been stranded in the cave was ruined beyond repair.

Susie had urged him to hang onto it. She was very good at repurposing things.

Hannah had insisted on sewing Susie a new dress and wouldn't take no for an answer. The pink gingham was flecked with darker pink flowers. Susie wouldn't say that she felt pretty, but it was nice to have something new to wear for this occasion.

All she had to do was say two words. *"I do."*

But those words spoke promises. Promises that she'd made once before. She'd kept her word, but Roy had forsaken his vows.

It had crushed her when she'd discovered his infidelity.

Could she trust Gil? A man she barely knew?

Gil looked over at her, and his warm, confident smile was probably meant to be reassuring, but she felt like a strong wind could blow her away.

He was too handsome, wasn't he? His cough had continued to fade over the past few days. She had explained the poultice away with a little fib, saying she'd remembered her uncle mentioning it before. She just hadn't told him her memory was very recent. She'd even talked Gil into eating two garlic cloves every morning. Had it really helped? Who knew. But healthy color had returned to his skin. A body couldn't tell by looking at him that he was ill.

What if he didn't die?

Maybe he sensed her panicky thoughts, or maybe it was simply time to get started. Whatever the case, he approached her and stood between her and Hannah and the kids. His body made a shield that gave them a modicum of privacy.

"Are you all right?" For some reason, his concern made her eyes smart.

"Maybe we shouldn't go through with this," she whispered.

She barely breathed as she waited for a spark of temper in his eyes. Or maybe he'd cajole her with smooth words and remind her of the promises she'd already made.

But Gil only watched her with unreadable eyes for so long that she shifted, uncomfortable.

"Aren't you going to argue with me?" she asked.

"I think you're arguing with yourself enough for the both of us."

She stared at the shoulder of his suit jacket. "What if this is a mistake?"

His hand clasped hers, and his touch was at the same time gentle and terrifying. "If it's a mistake, then we'll figure out how to fix it. Together. You have my word."

His words reassured her in a way she hadn't expected. He wasn't trying to sugarcoat facts for her. He wasn't promising everything would be fine. But he was promising to stand beside her. For however long he had left.

Her gaze fell to their clasped hands and landed on the ring she wore. Gil's grandmother's ring.

He'd given it to her after she'd agreed to his *arrangement*. But a ring like this, a ring heavy with family legacy… It signified more than a contract.

Roy had promised her a ring. Their wedding had been a few minutes standing in front of a justice of the peace. There hadn't been time to buy one— although now she suspected he hadn't had the money.

And her finger had stayed ring-less. Her marriage had been a sham.

Gil's arrangement was supposed to be artificial. A way for him to help Susie and her children financially.

But the ring on her finger made it feel real.

She wasn't going into this believing in a fairytale. She knew Gil didn't love her and she certainly didn't love him.

She didn't know how long their marriage would last.

Her eyes were wide open.

So she swallowed hard and nodded. "Okay," she whispered.

"We haven't talked about a honeymoon. Where shall we go?"

She hadn't expected that. "I've never been anywhere."

When they were courting—if you could call it that—Roy had listened to her talk about how much she'd wanted to visit the big city. She'd been to Philadelphia when she was all of thirteen, and she still remembered the wonder of it. She'd always wanted to go back. Roy had made more promises, none of which he had ever kept. He'd done all his gambling in small towns, claiming it was easier to win against country hicks.

Gil waved the preacher over. As the man approached, Gil mused, "What about Rapid City? We could start there and see where we end up."

He had successfully distracted her from her fears, and when the minister approached and asked if they were ready, she was able to nod.

At that moment, Albert began to wail. Even after a week, Hannah still seemed uncertain with him. When his cries only got louder and the preacher hesitated, Susie knew Hannah wouldn't be able to calm him.

Gil squeezed her hand—she hadn't even realized he'd kept it—and murmured, "It's all right if you hold him."

Hannah met her in the middle of the room and looked relieved to hand Albert to Susie. Hannah was returning to her seat when Carrie jumped down from the bench and rushed forward.

She stretched her arms up toward Susie. "I want a turn," she cried.

Over the past two days, Carrie's behavior had turned jealous. If Susie was nursing Albert, Carrie wanted to sit close by her side and read. When Albert was sleeping in his cradle, Carrie demanded attention.

Now, Susie needed to shush her daughter and send her back to her seat, but before she could say a thing, Gil had scooped Carrie up and settled her against his side, holding her with one strong arm.

"There," Gil said. "That's better. Now we're all one big, happy family."

Carrie leaned her head against Gil's shoulder, apparently content.

Susie found she had to blink a few times to keep her eyes from watering. It must've been stuffy in there.

There was no other explanation.

THAT'S Roy Crowell's widow. He fleeced a bunch of folks out of their money in these parts about a year ago.

The preacher's words repeated in Gil's mind as the man gave a short Bible reading.

When they'd first made introductions, Susie *Crowell* had tickled his memory, but he hadn't had time to figure out why her name had seemed familiar. He'd been too busy trying to survive.

He'd only known Roy Crowell by reputation, but what he knew wasn't good. Crowell was a womanizer and had been accused of cheating at cards. Gil didn't know if any of the accusations were true.

But a guy like that... he couldn't have treated Susie well. Was this why she was so gun-shy about marrying again?

He couldn't help wondering what had attracted her to Crowell in the first place.

But this wasn't the time for those questions. The fact that she had been married to a gambler before didn't bother Gil. He was nothing like Crowell. He had no need to cheat. Anybody could count cards, if they had the smarts and a mind to do it. If the other men sitting at the table didn't have the same advantage he did, that wasn't his problem.

He didn't need more money. Now that he had Susie and the two little ones to take care of, he didn't even know whether he would set foot in a saloon again, not if all he had left were a few weeks with his new family.

When it came time to say their vows, Gil squeezed Susie's cold hand in his warm one. He didn't mind having the children up here with them. It kind of made it better, as far as he was concerned. This was a commitment they were making for the children. It was right for Carrie and Albert to be part of it.

When the preacher asked whether Susie would honor and cherish Gil, Carrie's sweet voice echoed her mama. Everyone in the room smiled. And he pretended as if he didn't see the tears standing in Susie's eyes before she blinked them away.

He'd paid the hotel clerk to pick up Susie's trunk earlier in the day, and after they had shared a nice dinner at the hotel dining room, he brought Susie and the children upstairs with him.

Susie looked worried all over again, standing just inside the doorway, holding Albert and looking around the room.

"Albert will cry in the night." She bit her lip.

"It won't bother me," he said.

Carrie was drowsing on his shoulder. It had been a new experience to carry the toddler upstairs. Now, he laid her on the small cot he'd had sent up.

Susie didn't seem convinced.

"It didn't bother me before," he said.

"That's because you were sick. You were so out of it you wouldn't have known if the president had walked in your room."

He chuckled and moved to cup her elbows in his hands even as she held the baby. She didn't shy away from his touch, which was a good thing.

She was his *wife*.

He wasn't alone anymore.

The knowledge filled him with warmth and affection, and he bent his head and brushed a kiss on her cheek.

The preacher hadn't made a kiss a part of the ceremony, and Susie had been jumpy enough in the barbershop that Gil hadn't pressed the issue, even if he wouldn't have minded a chance to taste her lips.

That little peck on the cheek hadn't been the kiss he'd envisioned, but he meant it as a gentle promise. "Stop worrying. I knew what I was signing up for."

"I'm not sure you did." She muttered the words almost to herself, but he was relieved when she started to ready the children for bed.

A few minutes later, he lay in the darkness beside her, listening to her breathing. She was far too quiet to be asleep.

"You haven't coughed much today," she said softly into the darkness.

"It's been a nice break, but I'm not cured," he said.

"I've had a little reprieve from the coughing before. It won't last long. " He could still feel the pressure in his chest, an ever-present reminder of his impending death.

The consumption was biding its time.

Sometime soon, the fire in his lungs would return. Until then, he would enjoy the blessing of his new family.

10

"Carrie, be still."

Susie corrected her daughter for what felt like the hundredth time.

Across the table, Gil wasn't even finished with his first cup of coffee.

They sat in the hotel dining room in Rapid City. Carrie had eaten one bite of her toast and two bites of her scrambled eggs and decided she was full. And then she'd become a toddler-sized tornado, full of restless energy.

She'd fumbled her glass of orange juice and almost spilled it across the table, sent a spoonful of eggs flying onto the floor when she used her spoon as a catapult, and now she was attempting to stand up in her chair.

Susie's stomach was rumbling with hunger, and

her food was nearly untouched. She had Albert resting in the crook of her arm as she reached out to grab her daughter before she took a flying leap off the chair and landed on the neighboring table.

Gil looked up from the newspaper he'd folded into quarters. He took in the situation with a cursory glance and reached out to scoop Carrie onto his knee.

"You have a lot of energy, little one."

Susie sat frozen, braced for his comment to turn into a gripe. Would he aim the arrow of his words at Carrie or at Susie herself? *Why don't you watch her better?*

Roy's cutting words had always struck true. Should Susie reach over and pull her daughter onto her own lap? She was conscious of the other hotel guests eating breakfast, aware that she'd make a spectacle of herself if she made a grab for the girl.

But Gil tweaked Carrie's nose, and she giggled. He pointed to Susie's plate. "Your mama hasn't had a chance to finish her food. She needs to eat, or she'll get grumpy."

Susie made an exaggerated shocked face at him, but he only winked.

"Look here. Do you see how the carpet squares sort of make a maze?" Gil pointed to the floor, where squares of carpet reminded Susie of a chess board. Some dark, some light. Gil set Carrie's feet on one of the darker squares. "Do you think you can follow the maze around that table and come back to me?"

"O' course." Carrie was off before Susie could call her back.

"That's probably not the best idea," Susie murmured. There were three empty tables in the corner, so at least Carrie wouldn't be disturbing other patrons, but each table was set with fine china. What if Susie bumped one of them? What if she broke a set of expensive dishes?

Gil shrugged. "She'll be distracted for a few minutes. You should eat while you can."

How could she when her heart was still drumming in her ears? She'd been sure he was going to get angry with Carrie or criticize Susie's parenting.

It had been three days since their short wedding ceremony. They'd stayed one night at the hotel in Keller and then taken a short stage ride to the nearest town with a railroad. They'd traveled by rail to Rapid City and spent two nights in this luxurious hotel. The furnishings, the staff, everything was so much fancier than any hotel she and Roy had ever stayed in.

Albert was a greedy eater—that was good, because it meant he was growing—but it meant she was up several times each night to feed him. True to his word, Gil sometimes slept through Albert's nighttime feedings. The man never complained, not even with a sigh as he rolled over and gave her his back. Last night, it had been particularly chilly in their room, and she'd been shivering when she'd come back to bed.

Gil had gathered her close in his arms. She had frozen, torn between nerves—would he try to kiss her?—and relief to have the warmth of his body pressed close.

Before she could protest or thank him—she hadn't decided which—his breathing had evened out, and he'd fallen back to sleep. She'd basked in his warmth that hadn't come with any expectations.

And woken a ball of nerves as daylight crept through the crack in the curtains.

What was she thinking? Of course there were expectations. She'd been busy traveling with two young children. Trying to keep the baby from crying too loudly or too long. Trying to keep Carrie calm and busy.

Gil had been pleasant and patient with her and the children. But what happened when Carrie threw a full-on tantrum? Or Albert got sick and Susie had to nurse him round the clock?

Surely the man's patience would ebb, and then she'd be scrambling to stay in his good graces.

He liked her. For now. She needed to do everything she could to make sure it stayed that way.

"You aren't eating," Gil reminded her.

She gave him what she hoped was a friendly smile and picked up a triangle of toast, then bit a corner off it.

"Why don't you let me hold Albert?"

She glanced down into the sleeping face of her baby. "He hardly weighs anything. I'm all right."

Gil's glance flicked to her plate. Why was he so worried about her breakfast? The man had only ordered a cup of coffee the past two mornings.

"Do you never eat breakfast?" she asked.

He shrugged. "I am not much of an early riser, I suppose."

He wasn't? Carrie was always up at the break of dawn. Had their presence disturbed his routine?

Before she could follow up, he said, "You eat your eggs a different way every morning."

She blushed. "My late husband—" She snapped her mouth closed. Surely Gil didn't want to hear about Roy. Welcoming her past to the breakfast table was asking for trouble, wasn't it?

But Gil's eyes only showed simple curiosity. "I don't mind if you talk about him."

Her face still flamed, but she went on. "Roy preferred his eggs hard-boiled. I never really got a chance to try them another way. Growing up, Mama always scrambled them. Lots of mouths to feed and it was easier that way."

She'd been pleased as punch in the beginning

when Roy had ordered meals for her when they'd dined out. Even if the food hadn't been what she'd have chosen, she'd thought it was romantic. It was only later, when she'd expressed her wishes to eat something different from what he ate, that he'd shown how manipulative and controlling he could be. And then the money had run out, and there had been no more fancy meals. It had become a moot point.

"Do you have a favorite?"

Her new husband's scrutiny brought an awareness she hadn't expected. He was curious and he wanted to know her. Why did that make her feel so uncomfortable?

"I liked over easy with toast." She'd made a mess of the runny eggs yesterday at breakfast, but the taste had been delicious. "But maybe I'd like to try a few more ways. If you don't mind." She'd read about a fancy kind of eggs. Eggs Benedict.

Gil sat back in his chair, his smile warm. "I'll flag down the waiter. You can fill up the table with platters of eggs."

She laughed at the thought. How fanciful. And expensive.

"I don't think Carrie will last through an egg tasting," she murmured.

At that moment, Carrie ran up to Gil and threw herself onto his leg.

"You might be right," he said. "Besides, I need to go to the bank."

The bank. Was there anything more nerve-wracking than conversing about money? Gil had told her that he was wealthy. Wealthy enough to take care of her and the children for a long while.

But he hadn't mentioned buying a house again. And she was too afraid to bring it up.

"Maybe the walk will do this little one good." He tapped Carrie on the end of her nose.

"You… you want us to go with you?"

He looked at her with an expression of confusion. "Why wouldn't I?"

She could only shrug. She sipped the last of her coffee to hide her surprise. Roy had never shared about their finances. Oh, she'd always known when things were tight. He got quiet and angry.

But Gil was cheerful as they walked together down the street. He held Carrie's hand.

Maybe he would have them wait in the lobby area while he conducted business.

But no, Gil was welcomed by the bank manager —manager!—and all four of them were escorted into the man's office.

She was flabbergasted when Gil asked the manager to update paperwork to add her name onto all of his accounts.

All of his accounts—as in, more than one.

The banker seemed eager to do Gil's bidding. He even distracted Carrie with a piece of paper that had been folded into the shape of a flower.

When the papers were prepared, Susie signed her name with a shaky hand. *Susie Hart.*

GIL WAS INFATUATED with his wife.

He couldn't seem to stop watching her, though he tried to be unobtrusive about it. Like now, as they walked down the street after finishing their business with the bank. At least that was settled.

Susie dawdled in front of a bookshop window. What was she looking at? He studied her reflection in the glass, the way she bit her lip.

He was holding Carrie's hand—mostly to keep the girl from dashing into the street—and edged closer. Susie didn't seem to notice.

He felt like he was seventeen again, awkward and uncertain about what to say to a member of the fairer sex.

Eggs. His brilliant breakfast-table conversation? Eggs. How droll.

"Anything catch your fancy? Should we go in?"

She glanced over her shoulder, her expression registering surprise to see him so near. She started to shake her head, but he glanced past her at the display.

"You like dime novels?" He couldn't read the title from here, but the gaudy cover was enough to identify what she'd been looking at.

"The author is married to my cousin," she murmured.

Really?

"Let's go in and buy one," he suggested.

She wouldn't be persuaded, and they continued down the street. The weather was mild and they stopped at a park with a wide green lawn to let Carrie play for a bit. She scampered across the grass with her arms thrown wide as he and Susie settled on an iron bench. He couldn't keep from looking at her. The sun shining down seemed to spin threads of gold through her dark hair.

"What?" She glanced at him. When she caught him looking, she brushed the hand not holding Albert against her cheek.

He scrambled for conversation. "Do you ever miss home?"

Shadows tracked behind her eyes, and she turned her gaze on Carrie. "Do you?"

"I miss my mother," he said. "My father and I didn't part on good terms."

"Why not?"

"I've always had a head for numbers. You probably noticed. I was expected to work for my father in his railroad business when I finished school. Take it over eventually. He talked about his grand plans for me a lot when I was a boy. Sometimes I would go to the office with him." His father had liked to have Gil tally the weekly revenue numbers—a long column of tiny numbers on a page. It had been a game for them, to see how quickly Gil could add the numbers in his head.

He hadn't thought about that in a long time.

His most vivid memories were the shouting matches he'd had with his father on that last visit home. It gave him some warmth to remember that that had only been the end of their relationship, not all of it. He'd had good memories from his childhood.

She glanced to him, and he realized he'd trailed off. She waited for him to go on.

"At university, I found a venture I liked better than the railroad."

Susie suddenly straightened, calling out for Carrie. The girl had approached a woman pushing a tram. By the looks of it, she was chatting with the woman—a stranger to her. Probably telling her life story.

Susie called Carrie back as Gil was swamped with memories of playing cards in the university dormitory. How easily counting the cards had come to him. The camaraderie of wagering with his friends.

It was a fun diversion. Until it was more. He'd begun planning the gambling nights, arranged for food. It'd been too easy to win.

And then his operation had been discovered by one of his professors. The dean of the college had become involved. And then Gil's father.

And everything had changed.

Susie settled on the bench again. "I'm sorry for the interruption. Go on."

Remembering his father's ultimatum left a bitter taste. "My father didn't like my friends or my new business plan. He gave me an ultimatum. And I walked away."

He'd always known his father was a hard man. In business, no one crossed Edward Hart.

Gil had never expected the falling out. His pride had been stung. His father had always loved numbers—like Gil. Couldn't he see what Gil did? There were men just throwing away their money at the gambling tables. Why shouldn't Gil be the one to take it?

But his father hadn't understood. And maybe in the beginning there might've been a chance for reconciliation, but years had passed. It was too late now.

But maybe not for Susie.

He nodded back the way they'd come, the direction of the bookshop. "Your family means a lot to you."

She'd been looking at him, her gaze filled with compassion. Now, her expression went carefully blank.

"I could see it in your face when you told me about them," he said quietly. "That night I was so terribly sick. You miss them."

He'd also overheard her telling Carrie a bedtime story about Velma and adventures they'd had when Susie had been a girl.

"What would it hurt to visit them before we decide where we want to settle down?"

"It could hurt a lot," she whispered fiercely. He realized by the tremor in her voice that she was on the verge of tears. Maybe he should have left it alone.

He leaned closer and laid his arm along the back of the bench. He wanted to wrap it around her, wanted to offer her comfort, but she sat with her spine as straight as a rod.

"They might be missing you as much as you miss them."

"Or maybe they are waiting to say 'I told you so,' for the mistake I made marrying Roy. Cecilia told me not to do it. Not to run away."

She's been holding this in for a long time. He felt

the same trepidation as he might when a straight was about to be dealt to the opposing player.

"You've been reading the Bible to Carrie every night." He hadn't meant to listen. Something about the words she read had stirred them up inside. He'd borrowed it from her nightstand and read a little on his own one afternoon while she'd been resting with the kids. "Seems like there was a lot of talk about forgiveness in those pages. How come that doesn't apply to you?"

She used one knuckle to whisk a tear away, then sniffed. "Sometimes, what you've done is too big to forgive."

He didn't believe that at all. "Is that what the Good Book says?"

"No. I just know."

He followed his instinct and squeezed her shoulders gently. "I'd really like to see you settled before my time is up. To find a little house somewhere in a place you'll be happy. But there's something telling me you won't be truly happy until you've made amends with your family. Wouldn't you at least like to try?"

"No."

"Then would you do it for me? Fulfill a dying man's request?"

She shot him a narrow-eyed look that was partly a glare, but he detected amusement underneath.

"How many times do you think you can use those words to get me to do your bidding?"

"Just once more." He gave her what he hoped was a charming smile. "Please. At least give Carrie a chance to meet your Velma."

His intuition was pinging. Like that moment when he *knew* an ace would be dealt as the next card. His gut feelings were rarely wrong. And right now, his gut was telling him she wanted to go home, even if she couldn't admit it yet.

"You don't play fair, Gil Hart."

"Maybe not, Susie Hart. But I'll do anything to see you happy."

She looked at him funny. He braced himself for her argument, maybe sharp words. But they didn't come. This woman surprised him. She was always surprising him.

His heart thundered in his chest. He wanted to know her. Wanted to know why she'd made that face.

But she only settled into his side, silently, giving him a chance to close his arm around her and Albert and settle back to watch Carrie frolic in the grass.

11

S usie walked up the narrow aisle of the train compartment, holding Albert against her shoulder and patting his back in a pattern.

She'd hoped walking might soothe him, but he continued to scream in her ear.

Her son had been inconsolable during the train journey toward Bear Creek. She didn't know whether it was the constant noise, the *clickety-clack* of the steel wheels against the rails. Or maybe the overpowering scent of coal. It could even be the motion of the train barreling forward that upset her son.

It certainly made her feel nauseated. Every turn of the wheels was a reminder. *Going home, going home, going home.*

Why had she let Gil talk her into this?

She could still hear Roy's voice in her head. *Do you think they'll take you back if you leave me? You're ruined and you can bet your family never wants to see you again.*

She'd told him about the argument with her mother and the subsequent fight with Cecilia. She'd been shocked by his callous reception when she'd found him in a seedy hotel in Sheridan. She'd had awful bouts of morning sickness with Carrie, and when Roy hadn't seemed happy to see her, she'd felt as if she would throw up all over again.

Even though she'd had nowhere to go, she'd turned and stormed away.

He'd chased her. Convinced her they'd be married, though he'd been in no hurry.

It was only later that he'd used her words against her, reminding her of the break between her and her family. That they would never approve of her choices.

That they must've stopped loving her by then.

What was she doing on this train? Why had she listened to Gil?

She reached the end of the car and turned around, her skirt snagging on one of the seats. She jiggled it loose and winced at Albert's scream right in her ear.

She had done everything she could think to do.

Fed him. Burped him. Changed his diaper. Rocked him.

None of it had worked. It had been nonstop crying for two hours.

Thank God this train car was nearly empty. There was a man in a wrinkled suit apparently sleeping through Albert's cries. Another woman and her teenage daughter had moved train cars after the first half hour that Susie had been unable to calm her son.

Gil and Carrie were seated at the other end of the car, though she couldn't see Carrie's head above the train seats. Whenever her husband looked up, his eyes unerringly found Susie. The intent way that he looked at her made her blush. He was a puzzle she couldn't seem to figure out. He looked at her as if… as if she were the most beautiful woman on the planet.

She couldn't understand it. She knew what she looked like with her post-baby body and wrinkles around her eyes from not sleeping through the night.

But Gil didn't seem to register any of the faults in her appearance. He liked her just fine.

It unnerved her.

He'd laid out their convenient marriage as a way to protect her, to help her. But she knew that no help ever came for free. What did he want from her?

Since the kiss he'd brushed on her cheek on their wedding night, he had been gently affectionate. His arm around her shoulders at the park in Rapid City. Settling her hand in the crook of his elbow and keeping her close as they walked down the street. Another kiss on her cheek as they had readied for bed last night.

That kiss had been different. He'd tipped her chin up with his thumb and forefinger, and for one breathless moment, she'd thought he meant to kiss her lips.

His lips had branded her where they had landed —only a scant space from the corner of her lips. She could still feel it burning now. Maybe because he was watching her in that intent way he had.

Last night, she had been both frightened that he would kiss her and afraid that he wouldn't.

Her own tangled emotions terrified her.

In the beginning, Roy had been affectionate and passionate. He had wanted to touch her all the time. After Carrie's birth, after he had strayed, his interest in her had faded.

Susie had felt undesirable. After she'd lost the baby weight, she'd tried to dress in the types of brightly colored dresses he'd seemed to like on her. She'd made him special dinners and done everything she could to flatter him and cater to him. They'd become intimate again, and she had fallen pregnant with Albert almost immediately.

Roy's interest had evaporated again. She'd had morning sickness like before, only this time she also had a toddler to watch after.

She'd had to face the fact that Roy didn't love her. Not like she longed to be loved.

As her relationship with her husband had died— well before he'd perished—she'd thought maybe that part of her died too. The part that longed for a caring touch. The part that wanted a man to watch her with interest in his eyes.

But Roy had died. Not Susie. And it was terrifying to realize that she still wanted someone to want her, love her.

It couldn't be Gil, could it? He was dying. He'd leave, and whatever affection she felt toward him would tear her apart.

And yet... he looked at her like that.

Albert must have finally worn himself out, because his cries died down. He gave an occasional sniffling breath as he dropped off to sleep. Thank goodness. Her back ached and her arms felt like lead.

She felt upside-down. And a little sick. But she tried to smile as if nothing were amiss as she approached Gil.

Until she came even with Gil and saw the seat

where Carrie had been when Susie had gotten up to walk Albert down the aisle. The seat was empty.

"WHERE IS CARRIE?"

The alarm in Susie's voice had Gil sitting up straight in his seat, though it only took a second for her words to register and for him to relax.

"She needed the toilet."

Susie's expression didn't change. "Why didn't you call for me? She can't go by herself."

Now he was truly perplexed. "She went by herself at least ten times yesterday in the hotel."

"That was in our private room."

He couldn't understand why she was so upset. He'd purposely chosen their seats close to the tiny powder room at the back of the train car because he knew Carrie had to go constantly. "I watched her go inside. There's no way she could get out the heavy train car door by herself."

He had been lost in thought, staring at his beautiful wife, but he was fairly sure he would've noticed if the powder room door opened.

But Susie brushed past their seats and went to the powder room door. She knocked on it. "Carrie?"

She must not have gotten an answer because she knocked again. "Carrie, answer me."

She sent a look over her shoulder, and her eyes were wide and frightened. She jiggled the handle.

If the door was locked, didn't that mean Carrie still had to be inside?

The man sleeping halfway down the train car let out a little snore. Was he drunk and sleeping it off? He hadn't roused once during Albert's screaming, and now he was sleeping through this.

Gil stood and moved across the swaying car to stand at Susie's side.

If Carrie had locked herself in and couldn't figure out how to get out, then maybe he should go for the conductor. The man had to have a key, right?

"Do you want me to get help?"

She sent a glare over her shoulder, but he noticed the way her hand was shaking. "What I want is for you to be more responsible with my daughter."

My daughter.

The words struck true. He turned away. He'd thought they were making a partnership of this marriage. Hadn't things worked out these last days?

He knew she was tired and scared of going home. Albert's fussing couldn't have been easy on her. She'd been quiet and pensive all morning.

He rapped three times on the door. "Carrie, come on out now. You're scaring your mama."

Maybe he'd spoken too loudly, or maybe the baby could feel Susie's tension, but either way, Albert roused. He let out an ear-splitting wail, right in Susie's face.

She swallowed and blinked back exhausted tears.

This wasn't working.

When Carrie didn't respond, he wondered if it was possible that she'd snuck out of the powder room. Maybe she'd crawled under the seats and was hiding somewhere in the train compartment. But then, just when he was ready to take action, there was the snap of a lock, and the powder room door opened to reveal Carrie's mischievous face.

He saw Carrie's lips move, but he couldn't hear her over Albert's wailing. She'd definitely said the word *hiding*.

Carrie had decided to play hide and seek. And it was obvious her mama was worn out. That had to be why she'd made such a big deal of Carrie using the powder room on her own.

Susie's face was mottled almost as much as Albert's, her lips pinched. He didn't want her to say something she'd regret just because she was tired and upset.

He cupped Susie's elbow, startling her.

"Does he need changing? Or feeding?"

She looked at Gil with an expression of utter confusion. As if he'd spoken a foreign language.

He nodded to the baby. "Does Albert need to be

fed?" After three days, he'd grown used to the feeding schedule. He didn't think it was time.

If it was a change the boy needed, well, Gil'd watched her diaper the youngster enough times that he thought he could manage if he needed to.

"Let me take him," he said.

She shook her head.

But he'd sat in his seat long enough while she punished herself, holding a screaming baby. "I'll take a turn while you rest for a few minutes."

He reached out, but she turned her body, keeping Albert out of reach. "Don't."

Maybe he'd never held a baby before, but that didn't mean he couldn't give her a much-needed break. "He's not breakable, is he?"

She glared at him.

"I'm starting to think you don't trust me." This time he scooped Albert into his hands, ignoring the protest he saw forming on her lips.

He settled the child against his chest as she had and started up the narrow aisle, wondering how she had made it look so easy with the train jostling so much. He was afraid he was going to stumble with each step.

He'd thought Albert would feel fragile, but the little one was somehow sturdy, even if he was small. Gil's hands were too big, and it felt awkward to hold the baby against his chest like Susie somehow had, so he tucked Albert's head on his shoulder, right up against his jaw. He patted the little man on his back, counting off a pattern in his head.

By the time he reached the end of the compartment and turned around, Albert had stopped crying and had settled back into sleep. His soft breaths against Gil's skin warmed his heart with fatherly affection.

Susie and Carrie were sitting down. Susie was saying something to her daughter, but she looked up, and he would swear that she glared daggers at him before she blanked her expression.

He hadn't meant to frighten her—or rather for Carrie to do so. But it also wasn't fair that she'd snapped at him simply because she was worried for her daughter.

I'm starting to think you don't trust me. He hadn't planned to speak the words. They'd tumbled out from somewhere deep inside him.

Susie was keeping walls up.

And why shouldn't she? She'd told him only yesterday that her no-good husband hadn't even given her the freedom to order her eggs the way she'd liked them.

Gil was working from a deficit.

Maybe he should've expected to have a couple of hiccups as they settled into life together—short as it may be. He'd been a bachelor for a long time and knew nothing about kids. And she'd been burned before.

But he felt his time ticking away like the last few cards in a deck waiting to be dealt.

Maybe it shouldn't bother him that she'd said *my daughter*, or that she clearly hadn't wanted him to hold Albert. He could give her some grace, if she'd return the favor.

He carefully made his way back to his seat, opposite Susie and Carrie. He steadied the baby's head with a hand at the back of Albert's neck as he sat down.

Carrie had a sketchbook open on her lap and was scribbling something in pencil on a blank page.

"Give him back to me," Susie said quietly. She was simmering with temper. He could see it in her eyes.

There was no reason to wake the baby. "You've held him day and night since he was born. I think I can manage for a little while."

She opened her mouth and snapped it closed twice. Like she couldn't think of a name strong enough to call him.

"He's my son," she hissed.

"And you're my wife."

Her eyes flared at his words.

"It's my job to take care of you."

Her gaze darted to Carrie and then back to him.

"We both know that this isn't... isn't a traditional marriage."

Why can't it be?

The words stuck behind his breastbone. He had no doubt that if he said it aloud, if he expressed his desire to change their arrangement now, at this late hour, she'd panic.

The conductor passed through the compartment, calling out the stop for Bear Creek.

Susie's attention wavered from Gil to the window. She went pale, and he thought he even saw her lower lip tremble.

They weren't done talking about this.

But for now, time was up.

12

S usie stepped on the train platform with her emotions all in a jumble.

She was both frustrated with Carrie and relieved that the girl hadn't gotten into more trouble. And irritated with Gil. Her husband couldn't have known Carrie would play a trick like that. But couldn't he have guessed that allowing a two-year-old to go to the powder room alone was not appropriate?

It was easier to focus on her irritation with Gil than on his words.

I'm starting to think you don't trust me.

You're my wife. It's my job to take care of you.

Gil wanted more than she could give.

Carrie tugged on her hand, and Susie realized she'd stalled out on the edge of the boardwalk. She was holding Albert in one arm and held onto Carrie with the other hand. Gil had gone for their trunks.

That left Susie to stare at the town she hadn't seen in almost three long years.

Everything was different. And yet, the same.

Down the street, there was a hat shop that hadn't existed when Susie had left. One of the saloons had shut down, the storefront locked tight and a *CLOSED FOR GOOD* sign in the window.

Her gaze skittered over the hotel, where she'd spent those fateful first days with Roy. It had been easy enough to blame him. He'd taken advantage of her naivety, and he'd lied to her.

But if she were honest with herself, she could admit that she had gone to him looking for trouble.

She'd chafed under the small-town life, under Cecilia's shadow and Mama and Papa's protective care.

Those old feelings of not living up to her family's expectations led to a momentary feeling of panic. Her chest cinched tight.

He's my son. Give him back to me.

What had she been thinking, snapping at Gil like that? Gil was her ticket to freedom, and she'd risked angering him, all because she'd let her temper fly.

She had to remain in his good graces. It was imperative.

So when he approached, a porter with their

trunks on a cart behind him, she widened her eyes and gave him a warm smile.

His brows came together in question. Oh my. Maybe she'd overdone it.

"Which way to the livery?" Gil asked the porter.

The young man—whom she didn't recognize, thank the Good Lord—was pointing down the street when an exclamation from the boardwalk just past the train platform held her frozen.

"Susie, is that you?" a man's voice called out.

Gil moved to her side as boots pounded on the boardwalk. She closed her eyes for a brief second, not knowing which of her family members it would be best to see.

When she opened her eyes, Jonas was there. Papa's adoptive father. The man she'd always called *grandaddy*. He lifted his hat off his head and pressed it to his chest. "I thought my sight was going at last. It really is you."

There were a few more lines fanning his mouth than she remembered. A little more gray hair at his temples. But he was the same dear grandfather who had welcomed her into the family when Papa had brought them home.

She felt like she couldn't catch her breath. Suddenly, tears were smarting in her eyes. "Hello, Granddaddy."

She sounded breathless. Maybe because she couldn't seem to inhale.

He reached for her and she accepted the awkward hug with one hand, still holding Albert. He settled back, looking her over. "You are a sight for sore eyes. Your mama is going to be so happy to see you."

Susie wasn't sure about that.

"Are you going out to the homestead? I've got—" Jonas shook his head, interrupting himself. His gaze swept her up and down, like he still couldn't believe his eyes. "I'm supposed to be meeting with Sullivan over at the church. We're adding onto the building, and somehow I've been wrangled in to head up the project. But you don't care about that." He waved his hand. "Let me run over to the church and tell Sullivan we'll have to meet later."

It was the most words she'd ever heard Granddaddy string together at one time.

Grandma Penny was the conversationalist. Jonas was the quiet one. Usually content to listen, but when he dispensed advice, it was advice you'd better listen to.

Her presence had obviously discombobulated him.

Only fair, considering his presence had knocked her knees out from under her.

Gil laid his hand at her back. "We don't want to

interrupt your meeting, sir. We can rent a wagon from the livery."

For the first time, Jonas looked at Gil. Susie had always known her grandfather to be a gentle, patient man. It was a surprise when he frowned fiercely at her husband. "I suppose you are…"

"Susie's husband. Gil Hart."

Gil met Grandaddy's handshake, and it was impossible to ignore that the two men were sending a message to each other as they stared over their clasped hands. Jonas's knuckles were turning white.

It was Carrie who broke the tension. "Are you my granddaddy too?"

Jonas dropped Gil's hand, his eyes shifting to take in Carrie, who'd been half-hidden behind Susie's skirt. His gaze jumped from Carrie to Susie and back again to Carrie. While his expression when he had shaken Gil's hand was hard, it softened with Carrie. "That's right. I'm Granddaddy Jonas. What's your name?"

"Carrie," she murmured and then broke out into a smile. She edged out from behind Susie and twisted from side to side, the skirt of her new dress flying around her legs.

"You're a pretty thing," Jonas said. "You look just like your mama. And who is that?" He gestured to Albert, held against Susie's midsection.

"That's Albert," Carrie said. She grimaced. "He

cried all the way here. I don't think he liked the train."

Granddaddy seemed warmed by her chatter. "That's all right. Sometimes I don't like the train much either." He looked at Gil and then jerked his chin. "I've got a wagon parked at the general store. There's plenty of room for your trunks. There's no need for you to rent something from the livery, not when Susie's family is around to help."

Susie's family.

Susie didn't know what to do with the emotion clogging her throat.

It only got worse when Grandaddy stared at her for a moment longer, his gaze as soft as it had been when he looked at Carrie. "I'm glad you're back."

GIL'S MOTHER had taught him the art of reading a room at a young age. It had been necessary when Father had hosted parties for railroad executives or other businessmen in his circle.

Sometimes the room was friendly.

Sometimes, like now, the smile each person wore was a mask.

They'd arrived at the White homestead not long ago. Jonas had ushered them inside, where they'd been greeted by his wife, Penny.

Andrew, Jonas and Penny's twelve-year-old son, had bolted from the house.

Right away, Gil liked Jonas. During the wagon ride out to the family homestead, the man hadn't quizzed Susie on where she'd been or why she'd come back.

Maybe, like Gil, he had seen how close she was to breaking. It was there in the tiny lines fanning her eyes and the clench of her fist in the folds of her skirt. And in the way her gaze shifted to the horizon often, jumping around as if her thoughts were flitting like fireflies.

Instead of questioning her, Jonas had regaled them with stories of his daughter Breanna's life in Philadelphia with her husband and two young children.

His casual conversation had seemed to settle Susie.

Until they'd arrived. It had been only minutes after Andrew bolted from the house that they were descended upon by a horde of relatives.

So many that Gil couldn't keep them all straight.

Sarah and Oscar were easy enough. Susie's parents. They had three children. Leo, Julia, and Laura. And of course, Susie's sister Velma. She'd thrown herself at Susie, tears streaming down her face. The sisters had hugged for a long time.

Even Gil had blinked away suspicious moisture from his eyes.

There was an uncle, Matty, and his wife, Catherine. Matty was a sheriff's deputy. They had a couple of little ones.

Edgar and his wife, Fran, whose sister was Emma, who was married to Seb—Gil couldn't remember whether Seb was one of the adopted Whites or an outsider.

Davy and Rose and more little ones.

And one uncle who lived in town with his wife. Maxwell and Hattie. Doctors, the both of them.

And another—Gil didn't catch his name—who lived up north near Sheridan.

Since their arrival at the homestead, Susie had stuck close. He knew she was nervous, so he didn't mind when she leaned in and their arms brushed. He kept one hand at the small of her back.

She received a warm welcome. Everyone wanted to hug Susie and coo over the babies. It was only when Susie's head turned or she was distracted speaking with someone else that Gil received baleful glowers.

Like now. He and Susie sat side-by-side on a sofa in Jonas and Penny's sitting room. Susie was leaning forward to speak to her sister Velma, who sat on the floor with her skirt spread around her.

"Cecilia will be jealous that I got to meet the

babies first," Velma said. Gil had liked the girl immediately. She was vivacious and sweet, and Carrie had
latched right onto her. Even as Velma spoke with
Susie, she spun a wooden top on the floor for Carrie.

From across the room, Susie's uncle Seb stood
against the wall, his arms crossed, and stared daggers
at Gil.

Susie didn't seem to notice. She'd gone tense
again at the mention of her older sister.

"How is Cecilia?" Susie asked. He might've been
the only one who heard the vulnerable note beneath
her cool tone.

"She's well. She lives in Granbury."

"She's still teaching there?"

"Part time," Emma offered from her seat in the
chair across the room. "Her husband is the chairman
of the school board. His younger sister lives with
them."

"Really? Cecilia is married?"

Penny smiled softly from her spot on a long
wooden bench that had been pulled in from the
dining room. "She had a special announcement for
us when she was home at Christmas."

"She's expecting," Velma murmured from the
floor.

The comment was innocently made, but Gil felt
how Susie flinched, even if no one saw it. Susie had

missed Christmas with her family. She'd missed her sister's special announcement.

Maybe she had told herself it didn't matter, but obviously it did.

For a moment, Susie's tension was all he registered.

"I'm hungry, Mama." Carrie lost interest in the wooden top and tugged on Susie's skirt.

Susie looked chagrined, but it was Sarah who moved, stepping away from the wall and crossing the room. "I'll make you a snack, dearie." Her gaze cut to him. "Gil, why don't you give me a hand?"

The room seemed to hold its breath. Did they expect him to refuse?

Susie caught his hand when he stood up. He turned to face her, his body blocking her from everyone else's view. He was the only one who saw her discomfitted gaze. And the way her eyes widened when he leaned close to brush a kiss on her cheek. She was blushing rosily when he straightened.

He reached out one hand to Carrie, who took it and skipped alongside him as they followed Sarah.

The kitchen was large, which made sense if you had to feed all those mouths.

He wiggled Carrie's hand. "What do you think? A piece of cheese? Maybe some bread?"

"Five cheeses." Carrie held up a handful of fingers to show him.

He set her at a stool beside the kitchen counter, probably meant for working and not eating. "You're that hungry?"

She nodded vigorously.

By the time he looked up, Sarah was already there with a small plate and some cut up cheese and meat and a slice of bread slathered with some kind of jam. "My award-winning strawberry preserves," she told Carrie. "It's your mama's favorite."

Carrie immediately reached for the sticky jam. He could already imagine it covering her cheeks and chin when she was finished, but he didn't stop her.

Sarah slowly folded a cloth around the chunk of cheese. "Velma and I can make up a room. How long will you be staying?"

Her question was too casual, her attention on a menial task too intent.

"I don't know," he answered honestly. "That'll be up to Susie."

Sarah's eyes flicked up, and there was something sharp and accusatory in them. She quickly looked back down at the counter.

Some awareness prickled the fine hairs at the back of his neck. Susie had been conflicted about coming here. So far, her family had seemed welcoming. But was there something he'd missed? Something more between the mother and daughter than the tension of unmet expectations and secrets and running away?

Had Susie run away because of some cruelty from her mother?

Sarah put away the cheese and then folded a dishcloth on the counter. "I've missed my daughter very much. And I want to know my grandchildren."

There was some subtext that was beyond him. Was he supposed to feel guilty?

"You should tell Susie that. I know she's missed you, too."

"Perhaps it would mean more coming from you." She said the words quietly but had steel in her voice. "Since it was you who kept Susie away from us."

Oh. She thought he was the one who'd stolen Susie away? He had to admire her gumption in confronting him directly, though he needed to clear up the misconception.

But she quickly went on, "Susie needs her family. When she left, I..." Her voice broke.

He felt for her, he really did. Which was why he tamped down the anger rising at her insinuation.

"We had no idea where she was. We couldn't write to her. It wasn't right for her to leave like that. For you to trick her into it."

Was that how she saw it? That Roy had tricked or coerced Susie into running away?

A sudden protectiveness rose in him.

"Susie knows her own mind," he said.

He glanced at Carrie to check that she was eating. She'd almost emptied her plate.

"You'll have to ask her why she left," he said quietly. He could set Sarah straight right now, but he didn't know how much Susie intended to share with her family. He didn't want to make things worse for her.

There was movement in the family room, and he knew the time for this conversation was short.

"I care about your daughter a great deal. If you harbor bitterness toward her and what happened"— he met her direct stare—"you should know that I won't let her be hurt again."

A soft sound came from the doorway, and he turned his head to see Susie standing there.

How much of that conversation had she heard?

She was looking at him with guarded uncertainty.

He tried to reassure her with only a look. He'd pressured her to come back here because he knew how much her family meant to her. He'd wanted her to have closure, the chance to make amends with them.

But he wasn't going to let anybody break her heart. Not if he could help it.

Sarah registered Susie in the doorway as well and frowned.

"The baby will want to eat," Susie said, "and then it'll be time for Carrie to go to bed. Should we head back to town? We can find a room at the hotel."

There was a challenge in the slight rising of her chin.

"Nonsense," Sarah said. She glanced at Gil, and there was a beat of gentleness in her voice. "You don't need to stay in town. We'd love to have you here." She paused. "And I would like a chance to talk to you."

Susie hesitated but finally nodded. "We'll stay."

Sarah's expression softened, and she moved to embrace her daughter.

"I'm so glad you're back."

But Gil saw the tightness in Susie's expression over her mother's shoulder.

Susie wasn't home, not yet.

13

S usie woke with a start. It was daybreak, or just before. Her entire body ached with exhaustion.

And Albert was snuffling. Not quite crying, but he would be soon.

Her eyes fluttered closed.

He couldn't be hungry again. She'd been up feeding him what felt like only minutes before.

The thought of getting up now made her want to cry.

Her mother and father had insisted they stay in the family cabin. This was the room she'd shared with Cecilia for years before her sister had gone away to college. Albert's cradle was tucked in the corner, and Carrie was sleeping on a pallet on the floor.

Gil was far too close in the narrow bed. Right now, his steady breaths told her he was still sleeping.

Every time Albert had woken in the night, Susie had been unable to keep her mind quiet. Memories had swirled up, reminding her that she hadn't talked things over with her mother. Mama had been welcoming, but there was still a cavernous distance between them.

The overwhelming emotions from the day before contributed to her exhaustion now. She didn't want to get up. Her eyelids felt as if they'd been pasted together.

And then Gil rolled over in bed. His hand brushed her hip. "I've got him. Go back to sleep."

He kissed the shell of her ear and then edged around her out of the bed.

She would open her eyes in just a second.

She *knew* Albert couldn't be hungry, but she would gather herself and get up. Albert was her responsibility, not Gil's.

She heard rustling of clothing as Gil donned pants and a shirt. Floorboards creaked as he crossed the room to the cradle. He spoke softly to Albert.

This close to dawn, Susie had no doubt that her mother was already tending to breakfast. Velma and the children would be awake before long too. If Albert cried, it wouldn't disturb the family.

But she didn't want to wake Carrie.

She opened her eyes, prepared to push her exhausted body to a sitting position and then out of bed.

Gil had the baby tucked close to his chest. He cupped Albert's head in one large palm and swayed slightly.

Albert settled immediately.

Gil looked into the baby's face with an expression of affection so gentle yet so deep that it made something inside Susie ache.

She remembered a soft look like that from her birth mother when she must've been almost as small as Carrie. That was the way she had always wanted Roy to look at their children. Only he had barely ever spared a glance for Carrie, always too self-absorbed or too busy to really see her.

Gil had no blood relation to Albert, but looking at him that way... He certainly could've passed for his father.

There was something about watching a man hold a baby close like that... it tugged at her heartstrings.

Gil took a step toward the door and then seemed to realize that she was watching. He gave her a soft smile and then a wink. "Go back to sleep."

She considered telling him off for bossing her around, but when she blinked, her eyelids stayed stuck, and she found herself drifting back into blissful sleep.

When she woke again, the sun sent bright morning rays through the part in the curtains. She sat up abruptly.

She'd only meant to close her eyes for a few minutes, not sleep the morning away.

But the house was quiet, no baby was wailing.

Carrie's pallet was empty. She must've woken and gone out into the living room.

What would Susie find when she left the solace of the bedroom?

Gil hadn't been cowed by her mother yesterday. Neither had he balked when her uncles had been standoffish toward him.

It had made her feel as if…as if he was proud to be at her side. Proud of her.

Maybe the compliments she'd overheard him speaking about her shouldn't have meant so much.

Or maybe they meant more because he had spoken them to Mama, not to Susie herself. He hadn't spoken them to flatter her or curry favor. He'd meant the words.

If she took a few extra moments in the looking glass, securing her hair and then pinching pink into her cheeks, who would know?

After she was satisfied with her appearance, she let herself out of the room.

In the parlor, Velma was holding Albert, who was

alert. No doubt he would want to be fed in the near future, but for now he seemed content.

Julia and Laura, Susie's young sisters, played with Carrie on the floor. When Carrie saw Susie, she hurried over for a hug and then quickly ran back to her aunts, re-joining the patty-cake game.

Gil was in the kitchen with Mama.

Susie felt frozen until her husband looked up from the counter and smiled a warm smile that somehow drew her closer.

His sleeves were rolled up, and the muscles in his forearms stood out in relief. Were his fingers covered in eggs and sugar?

"What are you doing?"

"Your mother is teaching me to make French toast. It has eggs as an ingredient, but it might not fit your definition of eggs exactly, but I thought..."

His rambling words seemed almost...bashful. He quickly turned to the stove—was he blushing?—and removed a napkin-covered plate from the warming shelf there.

She'd heard his words, but in his flurry of action, it wasn't until he presented the plate to her with a flourish that their meaning registered.

"You...cooked for me? You made eggs?" She sounded as incredulous as she felt.

"Toast. In reality, it's toast."

But the flush high in his cheeks proved how much he wanted to please her.

He had.

In fact, she was astonished.

"Don't blame your mother if they are less than perfect. I burned the first batch rather badly."

There was a faint scent of something burnt that she hadn't smelled until then.

He was watching her expectantly while Mama stood at the sink, washing up some dishes. Obviously, she was listening. Susie could feel Velma's gaze, as well, from behind her.

What could she do other than try the toast?

Rich, buttery flavors burst over her tongue. She closed her eyes and savored it.

When she opened them, Gil was staring intently at her mouth. She reached up to dab it with the back of her hand as she chewed and swallowed. Had she dripped butter down her face?

"Well?"

She let him hang for a moment, tilting her head as if she were considering how to answer. "I can't believe how good this is." It was a risk, being vulnerable even for a moment. But she added, "I can't believe you cooked for me."

The warmth in his eyes lingered for another moment until Mama clanged a plate against the counter. "Oops. Don't mind me."

Gil whisked the mixing bowl from the counter. His eyes were smiling. "I'm told I need Grandma Penny's expertise for tomorrow's recipe."

He was planning more?

She didn't know what to say, and luckily her father banged inside, which caused enough distraction that only Gil saw her blush.

GIL WATCHED Susie ride a beautiful bay mare around the corral near the barn.

The morning had warmed up, and she was hatless, her dark locks falling out of their pins.

She didn't seem to care.

Carrie sat in the saddle in front of her, clapping with delight. Albert had been ready for a nap and Sarah had stayed back at the family cabin to watch over him.

Several of Susie's uncles and a handful of kids stood around the corral, taking in the sight. Gil had already earned his share of ribbing because he had declined when Susie's father had tried to get him up on a horse.

Susie was a natural rider.

Gil had never liked riding. He was more interested in the horseless carriages that he read about in newspapers. Put him on an animal ten times his size that could buck him off and break his neck? No, thank you.

One of Susie's uncles sidled close, putting one foot on the bottom corral railing. Gil wished he could remember the man's name, but there had been a slew of introductions, and he just couldn't get them all. This uncle had dark curly hair and wore a sharp jacket over dark pants.

"It's a nice morning," Gil said. "Remind me your name?"

The other man smiled. "Maxwell. My wife's Hattie."

Maxwell. The doctor. Awareness tickled the skin behind Gil's ears. But Maxwell didn't seem to notice his discomfort. He stared at Susie and Carrie as they passed by. "I suppose it's you we have to thank for bringing Susie home."

He knew Susie hadn't had the long talk that was needed to clear the air with her mother, but this morning at breakfast, his wife had admitted that her first husband had passed away and that Gil was husband number two. He'd seen the curiosity in Sarah's expression but Susie's half-siblings had been underfoot and there'd been no time for follow-up questions.

"I don't need any thanks. Seeing her smile like that is reward enough." He nodded to where Susie was beaming down into Carrie's face. He knew she still carried some tension. There hadn't yet been a conversation with her mother, one that definitely needed to happen soon so they could clear the air. But Susie was cautiously letting herself show little moments of joy.

Maxwell had followed his gaze and now wore a contemplative look. "Y'know, I only arrived at the homestead this morning. Pa tried to catch me up, but I think I must've missed part of your story. How long have you known Susie?"

Gil doubted the man had missed anything. His eyes showed a keen intelligence, and he had to have some smarts to be a doctor, didn't he? He was fishing for information, and that made Gil smile. "Long enough."

This time when Maxwell turned his gaze on Gil, there was no effort to hide the speculation in his eyes. "I suppose you were the friend she phoned me about two weeks ago."

Gil shook his head. He had no idea what the man was talking about.

Maxwell's brows jumped. "Susie phoned me real early in the morning. She said she had a *friend*"— there was no missing the emphasis on that word —"who had consumption and was in a bad way."

She'd done *what*?

Maybe she'd never planned to come home— never planned to get caught in the white lie.

"She told me she remembered you telling her about a garlic poultice from awhile back." She'd made it seem as if the conversation had been a long time ago. Hadn't she? His memory of the day after he'd woken was fuzzy. His body had been exhausted after he'd fought so long and hard.

Maxwell's mouth quirked. "Ah. Maybe that was it."

Gil shook his head.

How could he be angry, when her poultice seemed to have helped? His cough hadn't been as intense these past days. She'd reached out to her family for the first time in years because she'd been worried about him.

She cared about him. This was proof. Wasn't it?

Even so, he couldn't quite smile at the doctor beside him. "I guess I've got you to thank for that awful garlic paste?"

Maxwell smiled, too, something intent in his stare. "No thanks needed. Seeing you fit to walk around is thanks in itself."

Gil's eyes narrowed.

"You should come up to the clinic. I can give you a proper examination."

Gil shook his head. "I've had too many examinations. Seen plenty of big-city docs from the finest medical schools." A country doctor wouldn't be able to match their resources or knowledge.

Although, this country doctor had suggested the salve that had kept Gil from dying, something none of those fancy doctors had suggested. That was something. And he hadn't had nearly as many coughing fits over the past few days. Susie continued to ply him with garlic every morning, and thus far, he hadn't refused her.

The consumption was going to kill him. But if she wanted to play nurse, if it made her feel better to see him chew up those awful cloves, he'd do it.

He wasn't seeing her doctor-uncle in a professional capacity, though.

Maxwell's gaze shifted to something akin to curiosity.

Gil waited for the man to twist his arm or call him stupid. Neither of those things happened. Maxwell just went back to watching Susie in the ring.

Good.

He wasn't going to change Gil's mind. He'd settled the matter and was resigned to his fate.

Wasn't he?

Watching Susie urge the horse into a trot around the corral had Gil's heart rising to his throat.

Not because he was scared for her. Carrie squealed with delight, and all Susie's uncles and cousins whooped in approval.

It was the way Susie laughed.

Her face radiated joy like the sun opening up from behind an oppressive rain cloud.

She was so alive. So vital.

He'd told himself that, if the Good Lord had brought him to earth just to bring Susie back to her family, he'd treasure every moment.

But suddenly, it wasn't enough.

Gil didn't want to miss a single smile, whether it was for Carrie or for Albert or for Gil himself. He wanted to fall asleep with the scent of her hair for ten thousand nights, not for a handful.

Despite the promise he'd made after rising from his sickbed, he was falling for his wife, and his hold on the fragile acceptance was slipping.

He didn't want to die.

14

After she fed Albert and settled him in the cradle, Susie left the bedroom. From the hallway, she could hear Gil's voice and another voice that sounded like... it must be her brother Leo.

She waited out of sight, one hand resting on the wall.

Gil was...

The man had made her breakfast again this morning. Two eggs, sunny side up, and toast.

Maybe she was beginning to trust in his thoughtfulness because she hadn't been afraid to accept a meal with a smile. They had sat and eaten at the table together with hands clasped underneath.

Now she pressed her other hand against her fluttering heart.

She felt like she was nineteen again.

Naive and hopeful. Like she'd been before Roy.

Was it really possible that her heart was opening itself again? Like a bloom in the springtime, turning its face toward the sun?

She was growing feelings for her husband.

The same husband who seemed certain he was going to perish. And soon.

Wasn't she just setting herself up for heartache?

She was, and yet, she couldn't seem to stop herself.

She couldn't stop her gaze from careening to his when she entered a room. Couldn't stop her heart from pounding when he smiled his slow, warm smile. Couldn't stop blushing when he complimented her, often in a whisper while he was leaning close.

It was terrifying.

She both welcomed the feelings and despised them.

How could she dampen them, when he was so close?

Gil had been her savior when she'd needed one. He cared about Albert and Carrie. He played with Carrie and listened to her rambling monologues about her dolly or the kitten she'd seen. When Albert cried, Gil was the first one to scoop him up from the cradle. He wasn't frightened of changing a diaper or soothing the infant back to sleep.

He was a family man.

So why didn't he have a family of his own? He was a decade her senior, kind, and handsome.

He was too good to be true.

And after Roy... she knew that there must be some catch. She just hadn't found it yet.

She needed to guard her heart. For her own sake and for the babies.

A tiny part of her wondered whether she was overthinking this.

What if... what if Gil genuinely liked her and wanted to have a family for the days he had left?

She pushed the thought away.

Guarding her heart was the safer choice. It was her only choice.

When she stepped into the living room, she drew up short. Gil was there with twelve-year-old Leo, both of them on opposite ends of the sofa and two piles of pennies on the low table in front of them.

Gil was shuffling a deck of cards as if it were the most natural thing in the world. The cards slipped between his fingers effortlessly, shifting to the side as he cut the deck and folded them back into a perfect pile. The moment seemed to stretch, lengthen itself as she watched him deal.

The pennies made it look like...

It felt as if they were...

Playing poker.

She couldn't be sure. She'd never played the game herself, never stepped foot in a saloon to watch Roy play.

"What are you doing?" Her voice was breathless, which made sense because she couldn't seem to breathe. Every muscle was locked up.

Leo looked up with innocent pride in his expression. "Gil's teaching me to play poker."

Her husband tipped his cards up—they barely moved off the table surface—and checked them. The move was so practiced that she felt dizzy and faint.

What was going on?

"I thought you might lie down with Albert..." Gil glanced up and seemed to register the shock in her expression. His smile faded. He held out a hand to stop Leo from playing.

Her voice trembled when she spoke. "You're playing poker? But you don't—you aren't—"

Gil's brow wrinkled as if her worry didn't make a lick of sense. "I make a good living playing this game."

No.

How could he keep this from her?

Leo might be young, but he registered the tension in their voices and stood. "I'm going to find Dad." He scurried out of the room, the door closing with a snap behind him.

Susie's dizziness intensified, and she reached out

to hold onto the back of the nearest chair. It was an anchor, one she desperately needed as her life spun out of control.

"Why didn't you tell me?" Her whisper emerged harsh.

"Tell you what?"

"That you're a gambler!" Now her voice rose. It was as out-of-control as her emotions.

Gil remained calm, unaffected. She hated him a little bit for it. "I haven't made a secret of it."

She raised a shaking finger to point at him. "You *never* said you were a gambler. You—you said you came from a wealthy family. Your father the railroad tycoon."

She scoured her memories, fuzzy as they were, from the time in the cave. She was certain Gil had told her his family was wealthy.

He remained sitting, but a muscle jumped in his jaw.

"I told you my father disowned me. I've been making my own way since I was nineteen."

No. No, no, no.

"You saw the balance in my bank account," he went on. "That's my money. I earned it."

She pressed her eyes closed. "You stole it."

She sensed him jump up from the sofa, and she flinched, quickly opening her eyes.

His jaw was locked. "I don't steal anything. Those

men would come to the gaming tables whether or not I was there."

His self-righteousness made tears burn her throat.

I don't steal anything.

There was a rushing in her ears, and she pressed a shaking hand to her mouth, then her stomach. "I told you about-about Roy."

Roy had been addicted to the game. He'd been in the saloons every night, unable to think about anything else.

How had she missed it? Gil was the very same.

Her eyes burned.

Gil seemed unaffected, his eyes hard. "I didn't know your husband, but I know men like him. You know I'm not like that."

She shook her head. "I can't say that I know you at all."

GIL WATCHED the dawning horror cross his wife's face.

I can't say that I know you at all.

He couldn't understand how his profession was a surprise to Susie. He'd made no attempt to hide it, though he hadn't gone out gambling since they'd married.

He tried to understand how she could be hurt, given how her first husband had treated her.

But he couldn't understand her unwillingness to listen.

"I am not the same man as Roy was."

She turned away, pressing one hand against her mouth.

"Will you listen—?"

She flinched, and he worked to temper his voice.

"Will you... will you give it up?" Her question was quiet, resigned.

"Why should I?"

"Then I won't listen to you." She started toward the door.

He took two steps and reached out for her. He barely touched her elbow, but she went still. Her cheek was turned from him, as if she were bracing for a blow.

He exhaled a rough breath. His voice was low when he said, "I'm not going to strike you. Ever."

She kept her face averted. Did she believe him?

"Susie, for me, gambling is a good livelihood."

She shook her head slightly. "It's practically criminal."

Her words reminded him of the morning his father had confronted him.

It'd been two weeks shy of his twentieth birthday, and he'd been sent home from university after someone had reported him to the dean for gambling in the dorms.

Richard Price. It had to have been Richard, who'd lost two weeks' worth of the allowance his father sent to him.

Gil's father usually wasn't home on weekday mornings, but Gil found him in the opulent downstairs office. His face was drawn.

"What have you done?" he demanded. "Running a gaming den in the dormitory?"

Gil met his father's stare head-on. "Poker is all about probability. I figured it out during my algebra class. It's easy."

His father stared at him as if he were speaking a foreign language.

"I can predict when I'll win," Gil said by way of explanation.

It was far too easy to win money from his school chums. But after the school threw him out, he needed to hatch a better plan.

"I did not send you to that college to play cards." Father's voice was trembling with rage. His face was flushed. "What do you think Thorndike will say when he hears you've been thrown out? Or Hopkins?"

Gil didn't particularly care what his father's business associates thought.

"It's easy money. I'm going to play five nights a week. I can invest my winnings—"

"You'll do no such thing," Father snapped. He rounded his desk, opened one of the drawers as if he were looking for something.

"First, you'll return the money you won off your dorm mates. Then, you'll write an apology to the school."

"No."

Father looked up at Gil's adamant protest.

Gil was shaking with anger of his own. "It's my money. I won it fair and square. And I'm not going back there. Not ever."

His father had erupted, shouting demands and disparaging words until Gil had gone upstairs to pack.

His father's ultimatum that he return to school or leave the family had been the last straw.

This fight with Susie made him feel like that nineteen-year-old all over again. Furious that she didn't even try to understand.

"I can't do this again," she said quietly.

His gut seized. What was she saying?

"We—I rushed into this. Obviously, this marriage was a mistake. Maybe—maybe we can have the marriage annulled."

Annulled.

The ugly word stopped him cold.

He wasn't planning to live past the summer, so what did it matter?

Only it did matter. It mattered a great deal.

His body flushed hot and then cold all over.

"You made promises when you married me," he said.

She finally looked up at him, her eyes filled with stubborn determination.

"We were married in a barbershop."

"That doesn't mean we weren't taking those vows in front of God."

She shook her head, pressing the heel of her hands over her eyes. "I can't do this right now."

He was scrambling for some way to make her listen to reason when the door opened and Velma walked in, leading Carrie by the hand.

Both of them were beaming.

"Cecilia is here!" Velma announced.

Susie blinked, then turned her attention from Gil to her sister. He felt the cold distance she erected between them.

But he wasn't giving up.

He was going to have to find a way to make her see things his way. Because he wasn't letting her go without a fight.

ecilia was here.

C Susie was shaken and still reeling from her discovery. Gil was a gambler.

He'd betrayed her. He'd kept the truth from her.

She couldn't breathe, but Velma and Carrie were right there, watching her expectantly. She didn't even have a moment to compose herself. And *Cecilia*. She wasn't ready to face her sister.

"Albert is sleeping," she said. She couldn't leave him alone in the house.

If she stayed in until he woke up, she would have a chance to catch her breath. She couldn't even think, her thoughts whirling like a maelstrom. What was she going to do?

She didn't dare look at Gil, but she sensed him watching her.

"I'll stay here in case the baby wakes up," Velma offered.

She wanted to protest, but Carrie tugged at her hand. "Come on, Mama. Let's go."

Since their arrival, Carrie had blended right in, happy to be a part of the big, extended family. Here, she was never without a playmate. There were animals and lots of places to run. Susie had denied her this for too long.

Her excuses to stay and hide were gone, so she had no choice but to follow Carrie as she raced outside.

"I'll walk over with you," Gil said.

No.

The refusal died on her tongue. She was too aware of Velma's sharp eyes. The family was close. If any one person got wind of the terrible news about Gil's profession, then everyone would know in a matter of hours.

This was what she'd wanted to escape—the judgmental eyes of her family. The trapped feeling swamped her, stealing her breath.

Tears pricked as she followed Carrie down the hill toward the big house. She studiously ignored Gil, who walked at her side and slightly behind.

How could she have been so foolish? She'd let herself fall for him because of his protectiveness, his care...

But he was every bit the liar Roy had been.

I'm not going to strike you. Ever.

A traitorous part of her heart longed to believe him.

Was she really such a fool? She wanted him even though he'd hidden the truth from her, even though he was a gambler?

She wasn't only a fool. She must be the stupidest woman alive.

As they drew near to the house and the wagon pulled up in the yard, panic surged into a knot in her throat. Cecilia would take one look at her and know something was wrong.

Until three years ago, her sister had been her best friend. They'd shared everything. A bedroom. Clothes. Secrets.

Even after Cecilia had gone to college, she'd written often to Susie and even phoned when she could.

It was Susie who'd broken the relationship between them.

And now she had to figure out how to hide her tangled emotions from her sister. Cecilia had tried to keep her from marrying Roy. She had every right to say *I told you so*. Marrying Roy had been a mistake.

And now Susie had made another monumental mistake.

Why couldn't she do anything right?

As they neared, Cecilia was still on the wagon's bench seat. She wore a pretty blue dress, and the perfectly round shape of her stomach was adorable —not like the whale Susie had been.

A tall, fair-haired man was helping a girl of twelve hop out of the back of the wagon. Was this Cecilia's husband? It had to be.

Susie stopped short, panic making her breath short.

You never let me be the person I want to be.

The words she'd shouted at Cecilia almost three years ago in Granbury echoed through her mind.

She'd been a selfish cow, only concerned with finding Roy. Uncaring that she might hurt her family.

Cecilia had tried to reason with her. Begged her to stay, to come home to Bear Creek.

She'd refused to listen, and look what had happened.

How could Cecilia ever forgive her?

"Are you all right?" Gil asked.

His voice was low. He was standing too close.

Susie stepped away from him.

The weight of the past combined with what she needed to hide from her sister now swelled inside her until she thought she might burst.

Cecilia would never understand how desperate she'd been when she'd said yes to Gil.

She couldn't let her sister know. She couldn't let anyone know.

Cecilia's husband rounded the wagon and reached up to assist her from the conveyance. He lifted her easily to the ground, and when Cecilia looked up at him, it was clear to anyone with eyes just how deep her feelings for the man were.

Susie had never seen an expression that soft on her sister's face before. Was this really Cecilia, or was it an imposter?

Cecilia's husband bent to whisper something into her ear, momentarily hiding her from Susie's sight.

She braced for the moment when Cecilia would look at her. Her expression would change to bitterness. Susie was sure of it.

It was no less than she deserved.

But when Cecilia turned and caught sight of Susie, her eyes widened. Her lips pressed together, but not in a pinched scowl. More as if she were holding back emotion.

And then, she did something Susie would never have imagined, never in a thousand lifetimes.

She picked up her skirt and ran.

Susie let go of Carrie's hand and braced herself an instant before Cecilia threw her arms around her.

She could feel Cecilia's shuddering breath, and tears stung her eyes.

Everything was too much. The revelation of Gil's

true character still fresh in her mind and Cecilia's unexpected joy—a true gift... Susie couldn't hold back her emotion.

Tears streamed down her cheeks, and a small sob escaped. But there was no judgment from Cecilia in this moment. The two sisters were tied in each other's embrace.

Finally, men's voices registered, and Susie stepped back to mop up her eyes.

It was suspicious that none of the other family members—Mama and Papa, Grandma Penny and Grandaddy, or the other uncles or kids—were present. Had everyone faded into the background to allow the sisters their reunion?

Gil stood with Cecilia's husband, the two men visibly taking each other's measure.

The girl who'd hopped out of the back of the wagon looked similar enough to Cecilia's husband to be his daughter, but this must be the sister Susie's family had told her about. She was squatting beside Carrie, the two of them staring at something on the ground. A pebble, or a weed. Something that Carrie clearly found fascinating. The older girl was humoring her.

Susie offered the corner of her apron to Cecilia after she'd mopped up her own face. Cecilia accepted with a soggy giggle.

"I couldn't believe it when Uncle Maxwell

telephoned."

No one had said anything to Susie about it. Her family was never secretive. This knowledge, that Uncle Maxwell had phoned Cecilia, made uncertainty swell inside Susie.

Why hadn't they wanted her to know?

"I thought I would never see you again," Cecilia said. Her eyes were suspiciously wet all over again.

I'm sorry. I'm sorry for running away.

The words stuck behind Susie's breastbone. She was afraid that if she spoke them now, everything she was keeping inside would tumble out. That Cecilia had been right about Roy. That she'd faced raising two babies alone, with no money, and all the terror that went with it. The desperation that had driven her to accept Gil.

Gil.

She pressed her lips together, keeping the words from escaping. "I'm here now."

Cecilia's stare lasted a fraction of a second too long before she grabbed Susie's hand and looped their arms together the way they had when they were girls. "Come meet my husband."

Susie was introduced to John and his younger sister, Ruthie. Susie could see Ruthie's spirit by looking at her.

"Ruthie was one of the students in my classroom in Granbury."

Susie let her curiosity show on her face, thankful for a safe topic to speak about.

"I suppose you played matchmaker for your brother?"

Cecilia and Ruthie glanced at each other, and a secretive smile passed between them before Ruthie broke out in peals of laughter.

"It didn't quite go like that," Cecilia said, her own eyes dancing with mirth. "I'll tell you all about it." She pressed one hand to her lower back.

"After you lie down for a bit," John chided. He smiled at Susie, but his eyes seemed to see through her. "She was determined to get here as quickly as possible, and she refused to lie down and rest in the wagon."

"I'm not an invalid," Cecilia murmured.

"I know." The words between the two held affection and... a familiarity, as if they'd had this argument before. "But you must take care of yourself. You can catch up after a quick nap."

Cecilia stuck out her bottom lip in an exaggerated pout as John led her to the house. Grandaddy and Grandma Penny stood in the doorway, Mama behind them.

Thankfully, the family descended upon them, and Susie didn't have to be alone with Gil. She wasn't eager to revisit their argument.

As she allowed herself to be absorbed into the

family gathering, she couldn't forget the way Cecilia's husband doted on her. The man was obviously besotted with her.

Susie tried to squelch the distinct pang of jealousy.

Gil watched Susie from across the room as she sat and talked with her older sister. By now, he knew his wife well enough to recognize that her smiles were mostly genuine but there was something brittle around the edges.

He hated that he'd put it there. His temper had faded, and he'd realized that perhaps some of his words had been too harsh. Susie's disdain had made him feel like he was nineteen again, facing his father's ire and defending his life choices.

There had to be some way to make her understand. But not now, not when she was reuniting with her sister. Not in front of the family.

He stood off to one side of the Whites' large living room, holding a dozing Albert. Velma had brought over the baby after he'd woken earlier. Gil had been nearer the door, and he'd scooped up the baby because he wanted a chance to snuggle with him.

Susie had glared at him from across the room.

Penny and her daughter-in-law Rose and Emma, the dime novelist, had been working in the kitchen all afternoon, and savory scents were wafting in to tempt him. He hoped supper was coming soon.

Cecilia's husband John crossed to Gil, holding out a coffee mug.

Gil took it and thanked him with a nod.

The other man stood nearby, one shoulder pressing into the wall.

"I always need a little something to bolster me when we visit." John spoke the words in a low voice just before he sipped from his own mug.

Gil raised one brow.

"I don't know about you, but I find all the uncles intimidating."

Gil chuckled. He knew exactly what John was talking about. "You too?"

John's eyes tracked to his wife. "I had some secrets in my past before Cecilia and I got hitched. Maybe it makes me a little more squirrelly around her family, knowing that we started out with secrets between us."

Gil took a slow pull from his coffee. He hadn't kept his career a secret from Susie, or from anyone. No one had asked him what he did, and he had to wonder whether she hadn't said something to her family about his father and the railroad business when they'd first arrived.

Gil never made a secret that he earned his living at gaming tables. He wasn't ashamed of it. But after Susie's angry reaction, he wasn't in any hurry to spread the news around.

"Then again," John said, "there can be times when it's good to have such a large family at your back. A few years ago there was a bad drought, and the family banded together."

Gil looked down into little Albert's sleeping face. The boy was blessed to come from a tight-knit family like this one. Gil hadn't even known to dream of a big family. He'd only wanted to belong to Susie.

"Do you have a big family?" John asked.

Gil shook his head. "I've got folks and one sister back East. I... had a falling out with my father, and I haven't spoken to them in years."

John turned his way. He had felt from that first handshake that the other man saw too much. He was intuitive, could read a person's tells almost as well as Gil could. Maybe they were more alike than either one wanted to admit so early in their acquaintance.

Or maybe Gil was imagining the connection, not wanting to be the odd man out.

"My parents passed several years ago," John said. "There's a lot of things I wish I could say to them." Gil felt a pang of understanding. He wished he could introduce Susie to his mama. "What does Susie think about you being estranged from your family?"

This marriage was a mistake.

He heard again the words she had hurled at him. He shook his head to clear it. What did Susie think about his estrangement? No doubt if she understood why they were estranged, she'd agree with his father.

He forced a strangled smile at the other man. "We haven't talked about it much."

Maybe if they had talked more, there wouldn't have been a fight this morning.

Or maybe there wouldn't have been a marriage at all.

In his arms, Albert began to stir. The baby nuzzled at Gil's shoulder, hungry. It wouldn't be long before he'd be crying for his mama.

Gil shifted the baby in his arms, juggling the coffee mug until the other man took it from him.

As if she could sense that the baby needed her— maybe she could, what did he know?— Susie stood and made her way in his direction. She didn't meet his eyes.

John greeted her with a nod. "You'll have to come visit us in Granbury soon. I know Cecilia would love for you to be there when the baby comes."

Susie smiled tightly at him but didn't answer.

"He'll be wanting his supper," she murmured, reaching for Albert. Ignoring Gil completely.

Gil guessed John's sharp gaze missed nothing. His ears went hot with the awareness of it.

Even so, when Susie leaned close, he ducked his head to whisper in her ear. "We need to talk."

Her lips were set in a flat line as she drew the baby close. She shook her head slightly.

She never looked at him.

His temper spiked all over again.

He touched her elbow to keep her from moving away.

Did she intend to ignore him completely? Did she hope he'd just fade away?

She'd better think again.

He opened his mouth to demand she at least acknowledge him, but the baby wailed. Susie's gaze flew to Gil's, and he saw the despair she was hiding from everyone else.

Just as quickly as it came, she averted her eyes, hiding from him again.

His chest felt tight as she slipped down the hallway to one of the bedrooms to feed the baby.

He couldn't stay here under John's scrutinizing gaze.

"I'm going to get some air."

16

Two days.

Susie lasted two days until she could no longer keep her fragile hold on her emotions.

Mid-morning, she'd excused herself to nurse Albert. After she'd burped him, he was content to lie on the bed and stare at the sunbeams slanting in through the window.

Susie sat beside the baby and glanced at the indentation on Gil's pillow.

And promptly burst into tears.

She'd avoided Gil at every turn since their fight. If he was in a common room, she poured herself into conversation with Cecilia or her mother or Emma.

He'd tried to talk to her as they'd readied for bed in the darkened bedroom. She'd ignored him completely and then pretended to fall asleep.

Gil was smart, though. He wasn't fooled. She could see the simmering anger in his expression during the rare times she let herself look at him.

How long would they keep up this farce?

With the tense silence between them, her family must suspect. It was only a matter of time before somebody asked her about it.

More the fool, she missed their whispered conversations at night. The warmth in his gaze when he'd looked at her.

She could never trust him again.

She heard the door open, and she turned her back to it, blinded by tears. She hid her face behind her hands.

She didn't want him to see her tears and think she'd changed her mind about him. She hadn't.

But it was Mama's arms that came around her. Her mother held her as she wept.

And when Susie's tears were spent and she eased back from her mother's embrace, she was surprised to see tears on Mama's cheeks as well.

"I've been trying to let you come to me on your own time," Mama said. "I think it's about time we had a talk, the two of us. And maybe your sister, too?"

Cecilia.

Susie wanted to refuse, but she'd avoided this confrontation long enough. Maybe their relationship would never be what it once was, but it was time to find out.

"Not here, not in the house." She didn't want to chance Gil overhearing.

Mama's eyes widened, but she nodded. "The men are moving cattle today. We can take a picnic down by the creek. It won't take long to make up a basket."

Julia was sent to the big house to fetch Cecilia as Mama made quick work of folding sandwiches into cloth napkins and tucking them into a basket.

They met Cecilia in the yard. Ruthie trailed her, and Carrie was quick to run to her new cousin. Susie carried a sleeping Albert in her arms.

Dappled sunlight filtered through the trees that were only now greening up for the spring. It was cool enough that Susie was thankful for her shawl. The creek burbled and sang as it meandered through the trees.

The women found a place to spread the blanket.

It was peaceful, but Susie was too on edge to eat. She cut Carrie's sandwich into tiny pieces and then laid Albert on the blanket next to her. He slept without a peep, full and content.

After Carrie had eaten her fill, she wanted to take off her shoes and wade into the creek. Cecilia asked Ruthie to watch over her for a bit and reminded her not to get too far away.

And then there was nothing left to do but beg for forgiveness.

Susie didn't quite know where to start. Her heart was pounding. Her palms were moist. She clenched her hands and then released her fingers. She'd opened her mouth, sure she was going to make a hash of it, when Cecilia spoke.

"I'm glad Mama put this picnic together. It's been difficult for me to figure out what to say. I'm so terribly sorry for the way we fought when you came to see me in Granbury."

Susie was so astonished by the words, she could think of nothing to say.

Cecilia tossed a tiny stick she had been playing with at Susie. "What? I've been known to apologize before. On the very rare occasion that I'm wrong." She laughed a little, and Susie did too.

But then tears smarted in her eyes.

"I'm the one who should apologize. I didn't want to hear it when you told me I was making a mistake. I had made my decision, and I was determined to go through with it. Nothing you could've said would've changed my mind. But I was cruel and said things that I regret."

She glanced to her mother. "Mama, I shouldn't have run away. I'm so sorry."

"I'm sorry too, darling."

Cecilia reached out and clasped Susie's hand. "I

am glad to get the chance to see you and talk this out."

Susie's lip trembled. "I'm sorry I waited so long." She drew a shaky breath. "Roy was—" Her voice trembled, and she had to take a breath before she could go on. "You were right about him, the both of you. He was not a good husband. When I would've come home, over a year ago—he refused to let me."

In hindsight, she realized that if Roy had let her come, if her family had shown her this same kindness, she would've recognized the relationship with her husband was broken.

Had Roy known it all along?

Mama had fresh tears in her eyes. "If it isn't too much to bear, I want to know what you've been through."

Cecilia nodded. "Me too."

It was hard for Susie to talk about those early days. The ways Roy had manipulated her with his words and how foolish he had made her feel. She couldn't tell them everything. It simply hurt too much.

In the end, she was holding back tears. "I wish I hadn't believed him. I was so desperate to have the life I'd dreamed of that I wanted to trust everything he said. So I regret all of that. But if I hadn't married him, I wouldn't have Carrie. Or Albert."

Mama touched her shoulder. "You've always had

a tender heart. Always wanted to believe the best of people. There's nothing wrong with that. It's part of who you are."

Cecilia squeezed her hand. "And now you have someone decent in your life. John likes your Gil. He certainly dotes on you."

Just thinking about Gil brought on an onset of fresh tears. Susie tried to blink them away, tried to draw breath to keep herself from dissolving into sobs again. But in the wake of the reconciliation with her sister and mama, she couldn't hide them. Tears poured down her cheeks, and she let go of Cecilia to wipe away the moisture with her skirt.

It was several moments before she could draw breath.

"Gil is… Gil is a gambler, too." Just saying the words aloud made her break into a new sob. "I didn't know. I only-only found out a couple of days ago."

She couldn't bear to look up from the picnic blanket. Shame hunched her shoulders. She could hear Carrie's and Ruthie's voices, though she couldn't make out the words. The simple joy of them splashing in the creek was muted by her despair.

And then Mama reached out and took her hand. The connection gave Susie the strength to glance up.

Mama's eyes were wide. Cecilia's expression only showed concern.

Mama squeezed her hand. "You'd better start at the beginning."

Their patient listening without judgment enabled Susie to open up. She told them everything.

About traveling to see Hannah and the terror of the stagecoach wreck.

About going into labor in a cave in the wilderness with only Carrie and a stranger to help her. Cecilia's hand rested protectively over her belly as Susie described the night Albert had been born. She tried to temper the most terrifying bits so she didn't frighten her sister.

She found her eyes swimming with tears as she told them about nearly losing Gil in the small-town hotel. About nursing him back to health.

It was more difficult to talk about his wild idea that they marry so that she could be financially taken care of. How she'd been naive again. She'd wanted... she'd wanted to feel safe. To not have to worry about whether she would have enough food for Carrie. To not have to worry about whether they'd have a roof over their heads.

She was a fool for wanting to believe.

"I don't—I don't know what to do." She glanced up at the snatches of sky between the branches overhead. "Maybe... maybe the marriage can be annulled."

She had to squeeze her eyes closed against the sting of new tears.

"Is that what you want?" Mama asked softly.

She shook her head. *I don't know.*

"It isn't really about the money, is it?" Cecilia asked. Her voice was quiet.

Susie shrugged. "It was nice to be able to… breathe. But for a gambler, it can all be erased in one night." How well she knew that. "Not to mention that the funds in his bank accounts have been immorally obtained."

"Are you really feeling conflicted about the fact that the money could disappear, or that your husband could pass away?"

Mama's question stopped Susie short. Her chest cinched tight, and she felt like she couldn't breathe. "What?"

"Susie, everyone in the family saw how you looked at your Gil when you first arrived."

How she'd *looked* at him? What was Mama talking about?

"The same way Cecilia looked at John that first Christmas, the same way Emma looked at Seb…"

Mama thought she'd *fallen* for Gil? No. She shook her head.

"It was there in the way you spoke about him just now," Cecilia added. "When you told how he took care of you in the cave. You care about him."

The sudden silence was loaded with meaning. Susie ducked her head, tracing patterns on the picnic blanket with her finger. She didn't want to care about Gil.

But she didn't want him to die, either.

"Will he let Uncle Maxwell examine him?" Cecilia asked. "What if—?"

Susie shook her head. "He hates doctors. He won't—" She choked back a sob.

Mama shifted on the blanket. "It's all right to be frightened of losing him."

How had their conversation transitioned to this? Susie was furious about Gil's betrayal.

But her feelings were tangled.

She had gone into this marriage with her eyes wide open. Or so she'd thought. She had never expected Gil's kindness toward Carrie or how he doted on Albert.

Nor had she expected the way he treated her.

Even though she wasn't speaking to him, he'd brought over breakfast from the big house. It hadn't been simple scrambled eggs, either, but fancy poached eggs on a split muffin—eggs Benedict.

She'd pushed it away without even trying it, feeling selfish and mean, punishing him because she held a grudge.

She shook her head. "I can't have feelings for him."

Cecilia's lips stretched into a mysterious smile, a knowing smile. "Sometimes our heart and our head choose different paths."

"I have to think about Carrie and Albert. I can't…" Things were too muddled.

Mama patted Susie's knee. "You don't have to decide anything today. You should talk to him."

Talk to Gil. The man wouldn't listen to reason.

And she didn't want to have her heart broken all over again.

G il had made a terrible miscalculation.

He'd let himself be cajoled into accompanying the men in Susie's family as they pushed cattle from one part of their property to another. On horseback.

What had he been thinking?

He hadn't.

He'd been angry with Susie after she'd outright rejected the breakfast he'd prepared for her. He'd woken in the dark hours of the morning and crossed the yard to the big house, where Penny had promised to help him make eggs Benedict. He'd stood for a moment in the near-silent darkness, wondering whether he should even bother. He was making a fool of himself for a woman who'd declared she didn't want him.

But he'd decided to go through with his plan. It hadn't been easy, either. Discern the tells of five strangers around a poker table—no problem. Make *hollandaise* sauce—he could hardly *say* hollandaise sauce.

And then, after all that, she'd turned her nose up at his offering.

His anger and frustration had gotten the best of him, and when Oscar had asked Gil to come along to push the cattle, he'd wanted to escape.

He'd been a fool to agree.

Seb had been hiding a smile when he'd handed Gil the reins of a horse he'd called "green broke." After a few minutes in the saddle, Gil realized that *green broke* was probably a euphemism for *untrained*. He'd nearly been bucked off once, and the animal fought every single direction Gil attempted to give.

Storm clouds blanketed the horizon, and Gil had no desire to get soaked. How long was this going to take?

He realized he'd somehow gotten separated from the rest of the men. The hundred or so—maybe it was only thirty—cattle he'd been behind had lagged and started drifting away from the main herd. When Gil had turned in his saddle to call for help, none of Susie's uncles were in eyesight.

This was bad. This was very bad. How was he supposed to get the cattle to go where he wanted when he couldn't even get the horse to go where he wanted?

Was this a prank? Because Gil was panicking as the cattle spread out and wandered further afield.

It wasn't funny.

Maybe Susie's family had picked up on the tension between Gil and his wife, and this was some sort of punishment.

He pushed his horse to go faster and managed to bring two cows back to the herd—only to look up and find that five more had wandered off in different directions.

This was hopeless.

His shoulders drooped. Maybe he should ride away. Give up. The men of the White's ranch would surely come and round up the missing cattle eventually.

Maybe Gil should give up on Susie too. After three days of giving him the cold shoulder, she hadn't relented at all. She might even out-stubborn Gil's father.

Gil had thought something was growing between Susie and him. Maybe he was too much of a romantic, but he'd fallen for her. Hard. Why couldn't she give a little? Why wouldn't she even try to understand his position?

She wouldn't even *talk* to him.

And he had so little time left.

Though, his chest had seemed remarkably clear the past few days. He'd continued with the stupid garlic cloves even though Susie hadn't forced them on him like usual. It was silly, but he did it for her, even though she wasn't talking to him.

He wanted to see her eyes crinkle with humor when he grimaced at the flavor of the raw garlic.

He wanted her to look at him the soft way she had before everything had gone wrong.

No. He wasn't ready to give up yet. Susie was worth fighting for.

At least two dozen cattle had pushed toward some trees along the bank of a meandering creek. Unless Gil had gotten totally turned around, the homestead was somewhere beyond the creek. He rounded the outer edge of the cattle, knowing he needed to turn them away from the homestead.

Thunder boomed, and the cattle panicked, breaking away at a run. Some instinct in Gil's horse must've come to life because the animal gave chase.

Gil shouted and waved his hat, but the cattle barely shifted. They were stampeding through the trees, their hooves thundering—or maybe that was Gil's heartbeat.

If they turned toward the house, someone could get hurt.

And then he spotted a flash of color that made his heart skip a beat. What was that?

Further ahead, out of range of the cattle mob, Susie and Carrie were holding hands, walking along the creek bank. He shouted Susie's name, wanting to warn her, needing her to get to safety.

She looked up and took in the situation in an instant. He saw pure panic cross her expression.

She let go of Carrie and took off at a run—headed right toward the cattle.

No. Heading toward the picnic blanket spread on the ground and the baby lying on it.

Terror took hold of Gil, stealing his breath as he saw the people he loved the most right in the path of the stampeding cattle.

Susie was too far away to save Albert.

The herd was heading right toward the baby.

No!

Gil kicked the horse, and its stride stretched out.

But it wasn't going to be enough.

Gil didn't know how to turn the cattle, even if he got in front of them.

He urged the horse to the left, the animal's shoulder nudging the nearest steer. It could only turn so far, because there were more cattle next to it.

It was too late.

Gil ducked beneath a low-hanging branch. Pushed the horse for more speed.

One stride ahead of the herd.

Two strides.

Gil was almost on top of the baby.

He twisted the reins to the side and flung himself from the horse at the same moment. He'd held onto a wild hope that he'd be able to scoop up Albert and scoot out of the way—but that didn't happen.

He landed hard on his left ankle and saw stars when his right elbow hit the ground. He grabbed Albert but there was no time to get out of the way.

He heard Susie scream as he wrapped himself in a ball around the baby, covering him as best he could.

The first hoof crashed into his shoulder, cutting open his skin through his shirt and vest. A heavy footstep landed on his calf, and he cried out. He was jostled, but he kept himself curled in a ball. He would not let Albert be trampled.

He'd die before he let anything happen to the precious babe.

Hot stinky breath and slobber sprayed his cheek.

He was stepped on again, the pain spiking and then fading slightly.

And then two whoops, and the noise of pounding hooves faded. He braced himself for more pain.

But a whistle rang out.

Carrie was sobbing. He could hear her now.

"Gil!" Susie's cry roused him from the haze of pain.

"Get on!" That was Seb's voice, and when Gil

pried one eye open, he saw the man had pushed the cattle away from the creek.

Gil rolled to his left side, every muscle screaming. His head pounded.

Albert was wailing. Probably from fright, but what if he'd been injured? He loosened his hold to check the child. He seemed well, but what did Gil know? It was possible, in his effort to protect him, he'd gripped him too tightly.

Susie crouched beside him. She knelt on the blanket, settling a terrified Carrie at her side, and reached for the baby.

Gil relinquished Albert to her. He watched as she ran her hands over him, testing for injury.

"Is he"—he coughed—"all right?"

"I think so." She was shaking as she tucked the baby close to her chest, rocking him gently to soothe him.

Susie's father rode up, dismounting when he was still several feet away. Jonas and Davy pushed the cattle further from the creek as Seb swung around and splashed through the shallow water.

"That was some fast moving," Seb said.

Susie's eyes, terror stricken, focused on Gil.

Albert had begun to settle, his cries quieting.

"Why did you... why did you do that?" Susie asked.

Gil didn't have a chance to answer.

Seb hopped off his horse and came to kneel next to Gil. "You're bleeding." The younger man touched his shoulder, and Gil fought not to wince at the stab of pain.

"And your nose." Susie passed the still-snuffling Albert to Oscar, who cradled him in his arms and gathered Carrie against his thigh. The little girl buried her face in his pant leg and sobbed.

Susie fished a handkerchief from a pocket and pressed it to Gil's nose. He hadn't felt it until now. But now that he'd realized it, it throbbed with each heartbeat.

How had it happened? Had he hit his face when he'd landed wrong off the horse? Was it broken?

Having Susie close, her eyes scanning his face as if she still cared about him, made Gil want to do something crazy, like take her in his arms.

Seb poked at his back, and Gil had to bite back a cry. "You're gonna need a doctor."

"What were you thinking?" Susie demanded.

"I know." He finally found his voice. "It was stupid. I never should've let the cattle get away from me—"

"That was our fault," Seb said. "We thought to have a little fun with you. We were coming up behind you, but not close enough." He turned to Susie. "We didn't know y'all were down here."

"We had a picnic with Mama and Cecilia," she

said. "They retired to the house but Albert was still napping, so Carrie and I stayed..." She turned her gaze on Gil again. Her eyes were awash with tears. "Why did you do that?" she repeated.

Seb gestured to the kids. "That was a mighty brave thing, wrapping yourself around the baby like that. He would've been stomped on for sure."

Gil ignored Seb, holding Susie's gaze. Couldn't she figure it out by now?

"I'd do anything for those kids." He added quietly, "And you."

Her eyes were swimming with tears, and she shook her head.

He didn't know what that meant and couldn't focus on it. The pain was making it hard to breathe. He closed his eyes and focused on inhaling and exhaling.

Seb said, "We need to get him into town to see Maxwell."

"He hates doctors," she said.

"This time, he don't get a choice."

Gil wanted to protest that he was right there and could speak for himself, but Susie's tears and his own struggle to breathe stopped him. His brain kept repeating the last few moments when he'd grabbed Albert. What if he'd been two seconds later? What if his negligence had led to the babe's death?

SUSIE HAD ONCE TOLD Gil about a time when her uncle Maxwell had patched her up after a fall. She'd told Gil just how gentle and kind her uncle was.

Gil had never met a gentle doctor—and he'd met his share—so he'd doubted her words.

Maxwell touched a spot on Gil's lower back, just under his ribs, and Gil had to hold back a yelp. His shirt had been ripped to shreds, and he hadn't protested when Maxwell had used scissors to cut it away.

He was sure the older man kept touching his skin with the cold metal shears on purpose, making Gil jump every time.

He definitely wasn't getting the same treatment as ten-year-old Susie had.

I'd do anything for those kids. And you.

Maybe he'd scared her off for good with his words. Seb and Oscar had loaded Gil and Susie and the kids into the wagon and pushed hard for town. It'd started to rain, and even though they'd been wrapped in slickers, they'd been good and soaked by the time they reached Maxwell and Hattie's home. Hattie had whisked Susie and the kids into an upstairs bedroom while Gil had been taken to an office/exam room on the first floor. Maxwell had explained that they got plenty of patients looking for them at home, even though the office hours on their Main Street office were plainly posted.

Gil hadn't seen Susie since they'd arrived an hour ago. He'd sort of hoped that she'd stay with him, especially after she'd clutched his hand in the back of the wagon all the way to town.

"You've got several nasty contusions," Maxwell said. "I'm going to apply antiseptic where the skin's been broken. Hate for you to get an infection. This might sting."

Cold, sharp pain jabbed, and breath hissed between Gil's teeth. He clamped down on his molars to keep from saying a word the other man wouldn't appreciate.

"Anybody tell you your bedside manner needs a little work?" he barked when the sting abated.

"Not recently."

Gil blew air through his nose. "We done?"

"Not quite. Take a couple of deep breaths for me."

Maxwell pressed some instrument to Gil's back. Gil couldn't be bothered—every movement was pain —to turn and see what it was.

It took a second for him to get his teeth unclenched, and then he did as the man asked. Even the slight movement of his chest in and out sent pain through him. He'd been stomped but good.

Maxwell rounded the narrow exam table. His expression showed confusion or maybe thoughtfulness as he asked Gil to repeat the breaths. He wielded a thin stethoscope that Gil recognized from other doctors' examinations. Gil went tense.

"Have you been coughing much the past few days?"

Gil shook his head. "It won't matter. The consumption has stuck around for eighteen months. I've had a couple times where it nearly killed me. Some periods where it got better. It always comes back."

Maxwell crossed the room to a small cabinet, and he put away the stethoscope. He took a minute to wash his hands and then rustled up some bandages. He didn't immediately approach Gil but stared at him with an expression Gil couldn't read.

"I'd be interested to have a chat with one of the doctors you saw before," Maxwell finally said. "Your lungs sound mostly clear. I can hear something there, like maybe there's some scarring, but there's no rattle."

What was he saying? Whatever it was, it seemed irrelevant. If there was no rattle now, it would be back. Right?

"What have you been doing differently lately?"

Gil scowled. "Susie dosed me with that garlic plaster when I was ill. Since then, she's got it in her head that I need to eat a couple of garlic cloves every day. I can't stand 'em, but I can't seem to say no to her either."

Maxwell's eyes lit up with interest. "There's been plenty of studies on the medicinal qualities of garlic."

Gil had been bled, dosed with pints of awful medicines that made him sicker than a dog, poked and prodded and more.

No way had garlic cured him of consumption.

When he said as much to Maxwell, the other man shrugged. "What if it wasn't consumption? What if it was a lung infection?"

A lung infection? None of the other doctors Gil had seen had even considered that.

"Your body's been fighting it off. Doing the best it could. Probably some of the medicines your other doctors tried affected it, but didn't kill it. But now..."

"Are you trying to say I'm cured?" Gil knew his skepticism was audible. There's no way Susie's country bumpkin uncle could be right. He'd been told by five separate doctors that his condition was consumption. And every single one of them had promised he would die from it.

"What I'd like to do is have you and Susie stick around for a while. A few months. See if your symptoms come back. Maybe by that time you'll believe me."

A few months.

He swallowed hard, hope coming alive in his

chest despite the stern words he was using to stifle it. Almost against his will, he asked, "Are you saying I'm not dying?"

Maxwell stared at him steadily. "Not right now. Your lungs are clear."

It couldn't be true.

This changed everything. He couldn't wait to tell Susie.

Except the heart that had risen to lodge in his throat now tumbled to his toes. He'd told Susie he was dying. That was the only reason she'd married him.

A temporary arrangement.

She was angry that he'd misled her about his gambling—even though it hadn't been intentional. What was she going to think when he told her his lung condition wasn't consumption?

This time she'd be right in calling him a liar.

Even though he hadn't known. He'd been sure…

He couldn't imagine a scenario where she would be happy about the news.

I'd do anything for those kids. And you.

He'd spoken the words in an emotional moment. But he'd meant them down to the marrow of his bones.

When she'd clung to him in the wagon bed, he'd even begun to hope that she believed him. That maybe she felt the same way.

If he told her the truth about his health, she'd keep on hating him.

Wouldn't she?

His head felt stuffed with cotton wool, and he realized his nose was bleeding again when something hot and sticky dripped onto his hand. Spots wiggled in front of his eyes just before he slumped over in a dead faint.

The rain continued, and Gil was in such bad shape that Susie decided to take Aunt Hattie up on her offer to stay. Both Carrie and Albert were exhausted from the frightening ordeal and went to sleep early in the extra bedroom upstairs.

Gil, who'd fainted on Uncle Maxwell's examination table, allowed himself to be put to bed as well. Maxwell was worried that he might have a head injury and asked Susie to watch over him in the night.

Susie could barely look at him. His back had been cut in two places, and bruises bloomed under the skin. She couldn't believe he'd sacrificed himself for Albert. Or maybe she could. She had the evidence right at her fingertips as Gil slept beside her.

She couldn't imagine a scenario where Roy would've done the same. He'd been a selfish cad. He'd never thought of her needs before his own. He'd never thought of Carrie's needs, and she had no doubt that if he'd survived to meet Albert, he wouldn't have spared a thought for the infant's needs.

But Gil had, over and over again.

She didn't know what to think anymore.

She couldn't seem to stop touching Gil. Every time she started to drift to sleep, she startled awake. She had a visceral need to make sure he was all right, so she kept reaching out to brush her fingertips against his shoulder.

Finally, he rolled toward her and gathered her into his arms. With his solid warmth so close and her nose pressed against the skin of his neck, she was at last able to sleep.

She woke with a start when Albert wailed for breakfast. Gil's side of the bed was empty, the covers rumpled. Carrie was missing from her pallet, too. Where were they?

Albert's cries got louder, and Susie guessed he needed the reassurance of being in her arms after yesterday. Or maybe she was the one who needed it. She fed him, sitting on the edge of the bed and listening to the house around her. Low voices came from somewhere down the hall. It sounded like

Carrie and Hattie. Someone was moving around downstairs.

When Albert was satisfied, Susie burped him and, because his eyes were drooping closed, laid him down and tiptoed out of the room. When she peeked in the half-open door down the hall, she saw Hattie and Carrie sitting on the floor, drawing on a slate. Hattie looked up and smiled gently, tilting her head in the direction of the stairs.

Susie padded down to the first floor and followed the noise of clanking dishes into the kitchen. Gil was moving from the stovetop to a small table along the wall. He carried a pot in one hand and a spoon in the other. He moved gingerly, as if every step caused him pain. With his back to her, she couldn't see what he was doing with the pot, but the spoon scraped against metal.

Just seeing him moving around, injured though he was, brought stinging tears to her eyes.

She wasn't sure he'd noticed her hesitating in the doorway. But when he'd returned the pot to the counter—each step careful—he asked, "Are you going to come in?"

"What are you doing?" she countered. "Shouldn't you be in bed?" Was he really that hungry? Why hadn't Hattie sent him up some breakfast?

"I've a little headache, but I'm all right." He crossed to the table again and this time lifted a plate so she could see what was on it. "You didn't try my eggs benedict yesterday."

She stared at him, uncomprehending. He'd made special eggs for *her*? Again, even after she'd rejected his offering yesterday, after she'd acted so horribly toward him?

"Come in and eat," he urged. He set the plate on the table and pulled out the chair with a flourish.

But he wasn't as confident as he was pretending to be. At his side, his hand was loosely fisted. He twisted his wrist, as if he had an excess of nervous energy.

There'd been no uncertainty when he'd thrown himself off that horse to save Albert. Her mind decided to replay a memory of those terrible moments, and she blinked to clear it.

Her heart was pounding. She could've lost her child in an instant. She could have lost Gil.

And the man was making *eggs*.

"Gil," she whispered.

She stepped in, but she didn't head for the table. Her feet carried her toward the man as if he were true north and she a compass needle. Though she wanted to throw herself into his arms, she hesitated. Like when she'd laid beside him the night before, she didn't want to cause him further injury.

He had no such compunction. He drew her close.

She rested her hands gently on his upper arms, still afraid of hurting him.

It was the first time she'd initiated an embrace, and she was still terrified. Terrified that he meant too much. Terrified that she was going to lose him.

He bent his head and pressed his cheek against her jaw. His breath was hot on her neck. He didn't move, just held her, allowed her to hold him.

"How's Albert?" She felt his breath against her skin.

"He was never even touched…" Her voice shook. Her fingers squeezed involuntarily on his arms. "How are you?"

"I'm all right."

She scoffed. She could tell he was in pain from the way he'd moved.

He edged slightly back, one hand rising to cup her cheek. His thumb swept across her skin, catching tears she hadn't even realized had fallen.

"I'm sore," he admitted. "But I'll live." Something flickered behind his eyes.

She didn't have time to wonder what. Not when his lips pressed her cheek in a butterfly-light kiss.

Her breath caught in her chest.

He brushed another kiss against her temple.

Her eyes fluttered closed.

One kiss against her brow, and then the bridge of her nose. And finally one at the corner of her mouth.

She held her breath, waiting. Would he kiss her properly?

She wanted him to, even though the thought of it terrified her.

"You're so beautiful," he whispered.

The unexpected words jarred her out of the moment, and her eyes flew open.

She shook her head slightly, a flush climbing in her cheeks under his intent stare.

She knew exactly what she looked like. Bags under her eyes from a sleepless night, her body changed by carrying two children. Worry lines and frown lines and wilted hair.

"You are." He kissed her opposite temple. Her opposite cheek. "And I'll keep saying it until you believe me."

He kissed the corner of her mouth again, and her eyes fell closed. This time maybe she turned her head or maybe he decided to finally take the initiative. Whatever the case, his lips closed over hers.

His kiss was both tender and gentle, as if he were trying to prove his words true with only his lips against hers.

She met his kiss sweetly. Beginning to believe him.

He drew away slightly, cradling her face in his hands. He didn't push for more intimacy, like Roy always had. Gil smiled and let his hand fall to close around hers.

"Your food is getting cold."

Who could eat at a time like this? Her pulse was racing, her mind replaying the memory of his kiss.

He squeezed her hand. "I worked hard on those eggs," he teased.

She let him settle her into the chair. He moved his closer so they sat side-by-side instead of facing each other.

She could see the effort he'd put in, even though the bread was toasted unevenly and one of the eggs had broken and yolk ran down the side of the toast. The hollandaise sauce was a splash of bright yellow against the white plate.

"It's supposed to be a muffin, but bread was the best I could do on short notice."

Was he really apologizing that it was imperfect?

"It's lovely," she murmured. "But Gil?" Why had he done it? His selfless actions yesterday had shown just how deeply he cared for Albert—and for her. Making breakfast because of a silly whim she'd had…

That was something altogether more. Something that both cinched her chest tightly and made her feel as if she were flying.

"I'm not ready to give up on us," he said quietly, his voice full of determination.

Fresh tears stung her eyes. Staring at the eggs was easier than looking at her husband. "Gil, I—"

Her hand fisted around the spoon. Gil's larger hand covered her wrist and gently clasped her clenched fingers. "I was too proud. Before. I didn't really listen to you. I didn't try to understand what you'd been through. But I'm listening now."

Was he talking about...? He wanted to know what her life with Roy had been like?

Her appetite fled completely. She shook her head. "I don't like talking about it." She didn't like thinking about it, remembering...

But Gil waited patiently. After everything that had happened, didn't he deserve to know?

"There were times when Roy was on top of the world—when he'd hit a good streak." She stared at the plate in front of her without really seeing it. "There were times when his losing streak never seemed to end. Times when there was no money at all. No food in the house." She swallowed hard, remembering a time just after Carrie had started eating solid foods. How Susie's stomach had gnawed at her insides, how she'd felt faint with hunger. But Carrie had needed to eat, and there hadn't been enough.

Susie'd been terrified at the thought of her daughter's hunger.

Gil squeezed her hand gently, bringing her back

to the present. "You've got access to our bank accounts."

But what about when the accounts were empty? What then?

"It wasn't only about the money," she said, her words faltering. Again, Gil waited her out. "Roy always chased the next thrill. Whether it was a high-stakes game or... another woman."

Gil went very still beside her.

Thinking about it still ripped her insides to shreds. Why hadn't she been enough?

"Every night when he left for the tables, I would wonder who was sitting beside him."

She turned her face to the side, shame flushing her skin. But this had to be said. "I don't—I can't do it again."

She hadn't meant to, but she'd lost her heart to Gil. What she felt for him was deeper, purer than what she'd felt for Roy. If Gil came home smelling of another woman's perfume... It would break her.

When he spoke, Gil's voice vibrated with anger. "I cannot understand how he had a treasure like you and squandered it."

Just like when he'd called her beautiful, his words now caused her to shake her head. "I'm not—"

"You are a treasure," he said firmly. "And I'd like to think I'm more intelligent than that swine."

Now she glanced at Gil, unable to keep her lips from twitching as she fought a smile.

He was watching her without a trace of pity. If anything, there was pride shining in his eyes. For her? But... why?

"Yesterday I said I'd do anything for you and the kids. I meant it. That includes giving up a lifestyle that would hurt you."

She swallowed hard.

"I'd already decided. Everything you told me just now only solidified my resolve."

She searched his face. He was sincere, determination pouring off of him.

"I don't need more money. And I don't need to chase any thrills. Everything I need is under this roof. It's you and the kids."

His words were exactly the reassurance she needed. But...

When she'd seen the cattle stampeding toward Gil, she'd thought he was lost to her. Last night as he'd held her in bed, she'd been reminded that their time together was a ticking clock.

How could she bear to lose him all over again?

Now she dropped her gaze. "I-I care about you." It was a lie. She'd gone far past caring. She was desperately in love with him. "I don't know if I can bear to lose you. Maybe it's best if we don't allow ourselves to grow any closer."

Even as she said the words, she wanted to call them back. Was she really a coward?

If she was smart, she'd hold on to every moment they had left.

"I DIDN'T MEAN THAT."

Susie's words, uttered in a rush only a moment after her pronouncement, allowed Gil to begin to breathe again.

"I'm just... it's frightening to think of losing you." Susie's eyes swam with tears.

"Come here."

He stood, abused muscles in his back protesting, and drew her into his arms. Where she belonged. She was trembling, and he rubbed her back in soothing strokes. He never wanted to let her go.

"I've never intentionally lied to you," he started.

She drew back, and her eyes swept over his face.

"Last night, your uncle examined me and when he listened to my lungs, they were clear."

His heart was in his throat. Would she give him a chance to explain? He'd just declared his devotion to her, and he'd meant the words with all his heart. He prayed she'd believe them. "It seems that the doctors I saw before—all five of them—were mistaken in their diagnosis. Your uncle doesn't believe I have consumption at all."

She was still staring at him, clearly bewildered. "But... you nearly died. I was there with you. You couldn't breathe."

At her words, his body took a deep breath as if in protest of the memory of that night. He'd been sure he was a goner. "I know. Your uncle said that it might've been a lingering lung infection. One that you cured with your garlic poultice and the disgusting raw garlic you forced me to eat."

Her eyes lit up. "I cured you?"

"Unwittingly."

She snickered, and he chuckled.

But when her smile faded and she became thoughtful, he rushed on. "I never meant to mislead you. Or trap you in marriage."

"You aren't dying." Her words were filled with the same disbelief that had overcome him last night.

"Your uncle doesn't seem to think so."

She raised one expressive brow. "You trust him?"

"For a doctor, he isn't so bad. He said time will tell. If the lung infection doesn't return in the next few months, it may be gone forever."

Her eyes were soft, and he took heart in the fact that she was still in his embrace.

"There is one more thing," he said. "I made one promise to you that I can't keep."

Her breath stuttered.

His pulse pounded in his ears. He was all in without really knowing her hand. "I promised I wouldn't fall in love with you, but I have."

Her eyes softened and that gave him the courage to go on. "I don't want an annulment. I want a real marriage. With you. One that lasts a lifetime."

"A lifetime of garlic cloves for breakfast?" she teased.

He tweaked her nose. "A lifetime of eggs for breakfast."

She wrinkled her nose at him. "Are there that many recipes?"

"Probably not."

She considered him. But then she bit her lip. "I'm sorry."

His heart dropped to his toes. Was she rejecting him? But no, she wasn't pushing him away.

She glanced at the plate abandoned on the table. "They've gotten cold."

The eggs.

He held her gaze. "I'll make more. Today. And tomorrow. And for all our tomorrows." His humor faded away. "I love you, Susie. We haven't known each other long, but I'll prove it to you every day."

She blinked, and her eyes were suspiciously shiny. "I love you too," she whispered.

His own eyes were suddenly wet, so he closed

them as he kissed her. He'd dreamed of this kiss for almost as long as he'd known her. With each tender touch, he attempted to show her the truth of his words. *I love you, I love you, I love you.*

When he finally raised his head, her lips were bee-stung, and he was panting for breath.

His heart felt full to bursting. "There's one more thing."

Her eyes narrowed.

"I think we should get married. In a church this time, with all your family there."

Susie's lips trembled, and he worried he'd said the wrong thing.

"I'm not sure you understand what an undertaking that would be," she murmured.

He eased back a little, linking his hands around her waist. "Oh, I understand. It'll mean your uncles giving me a hard time. Your mama will want to sew you a new dress, and we'll have to coordinate with Cecilia to make sure she can be here to stand up with you. There will be flowers and a big meal, and things will probably get a little crazy."

She nodded, biting her lip. A smile was hiding around the corners of her mouth.

He kissed the very tip of her nose. "I wouldn't have it any other way."

EPILOGUE

Walt took aim and fired. The bullet nicked the tin can he had set on the stump of a tree several dozen yards away but didn't topple it.

"Pretty good," said a voice from behind him.

"Thanks." He waited a moment before he turned.

He'd been tracking the young man's progress as he'd skirted the edge of the field, sticking to the tree line that followed the little creek, off to one side and behind Walt. Out of range from Walt's target.

Walt was pretty sure he didn't know the man, but he couldn't be sure until he got closer.

Which he was doing as he waltzed toward him.

Walt took stock of him in one glance. Probably close to Walt's eighteen years. Dressed like a cowpoke in brown pants and a blue shirt and a battered hat that'd seen better days. Clean-shaven with clear blue eyes that took Walt's measure right back.

And then he grinned. "You a lawman?"

Awareness tingled at the back of Walt's neck. It was a weird question to ask on a first meeting. Why would someone ask that, unless he wasn't a law-abiding citizen?

"Naw." But his brother was. Matty was a sheriff's deputy and Walt's hero. He'd once interrupted a bank robbery and saved a bunch of folks. "Just practicin' for a sharpshooter competition. Part of the Founder's Day celebration in a few weeks."

Usually the town's big to-do was just a parade, a picnic, and a basket auction for the young women. When Walt had heard about the new sharpshooter competition, he'd been elated.

"Sharpshooter competition, huh? What's the prize?"

"A saddle, I think."

Walt didn't care about the saddle. He was excited about the chance to show his older brother and his pa that he was ready to put on the badge.

Walt wanted to be just like his older brother. Far as he was concerned, it was only a matter of time.

He squinted in an exaggerated way. "You a lawman?"

The newcomer guffawed. "No. Name's Tom

Harris. I hired on with a ranch over yonder. Big spread." He jerked his thumb behind him.

"The Beller place?"

Tom's eyes sparked. "That's the one."

It was strange that Tom was on foot. Where was his horse? But Walt's ma had preached politeness his entire life, and he didn't want to be rude.

"I'm Walt White." He extended his hand and shook Tom's. "My pa owns this land." The homestead stretched farther than a body could see, but Walt figured that said enough.

"Real pretty around these parts," Tom said.

Walt let his eyes roam to the horizon. The Laramie Mountains rose purple in the distance. He knew every bird call and every animal on the ranch, every twist of the creek and every gully where a calving heifer could hide.

He loved his home.

But there was a part of him that longed to see more of the world. His older sister Breanna had been badgering him to visit her family in Philadelphia. Maybe after his birthday, he'd take her up on it. Or maybe he'd stay, if Matty could get him on as a deputy. Not that Matty seemed in any hurry, even though Walt asked him every time they met up.

"You mind if I have a go?" Tom gestured at Walt's pistol.

Walt hesitated. If Tom'd been any of his neighbors, he wouldn't have minded. But they'd only just met.

He figured it didn't hurt none.

He handed Tom the weapon by its butt, and the other man flipped open the cylinder and checked the chambers before closing it back into place. His movements were smooth and sure, even though he'd never held that weapon before.

Tom lifted the gun and fired off all the rounds in quick order. The first two hit the can, the third knocked it off the stump and into the air. The last three hit it while it was in the air.

Walt stared in shock. "How'd you do that?"

His new friend handed the gun back with a grin. "My older brother is something of a sharpshooter. I learned from him." There was someone out there *better* than Tom? Walt would pay good money to see that.

"Can you teach me?"

Tom's gaze sharpened on the horizon. Walt glanced that way. Maybe that was the twitch of a horse's tail moving just out of sight. Or maybe it had been nothing.

When he looked back at Walt, he smiled widely. "Maybe another time. Gotta get back to the spread or the foreman'll be on my case."

"Are you sticking around Bear Creek?"

Tom shrugged. "For a while. Thanks for letting

me play."

"Do me a favor, will you?" Walt called as his new friend walked off the direction he'd come from.

Tom glanced over his shoulder.

"Don't come to town on Founder's Day. And don't enter the sharpshooter competition!"

Tom just laughed as he walked out of sight.

A week later, Walt had been tasked with accompanying his sister Ida and cousins Julia and Laura into town. Ma and Aunt Cecilia had agreed to let them each purchase a store-bought dress as a special treat for the upcoming Founder's Day events.

He'd been standing on the boardwalk in the hot sun for what seemed like hours. Just how long did it take to pick out a dress?

He crossed his arms, leaning his hip against the family wagon parked beside the boardwalk. He nodded to his former schoolteacher and to one of his ma's friends going into the grocery down the street. And there was the suspicious character again.

The same man in a sharp, black derby had walked past the bank twice in the last few minutes. He wore cowhand duds, dusty pants, a worn shirt, and a dark vest. He was scruffy, with a jaw that hadn't seen a shave in several days.

He stopped in the shade of the alley between the bank and the mercantile. He stood for a long time peering into the shadows between the two buildings before he scooted to one side and leaned his shoulder against the corner of the building.

Walt didn't blame him for seeking out some shade on this hot afternoon.

But it was certainly strange the way he kept looking around.

Suspicious, even.

A prickle of unease tickled the hair at the nape of Walt's neck. Last night, Matty and Catherine and their two kids had been over for supper. After the meal, Walt had been washing up with Ma and over-heard Matty and Pa talking about the Seymour gang. Apparently, the sheriff's office had received a wire that the gang might be in the area.

The Seymour gang had been in the newspapers for months. They were a group of six to ten men who'd been accused of a bank robbery in Steamboat Springs, Colorado, a train robbery near Ogden, Utah, and several stage robberies across Montana and Idaho.

If the Seymour gang had migrated to Wyoming, it couldn't be good.

Walt's uncle Sam managed the Bear Creek Bank and had since Walt was a little tyke. If he got caught in the crossfire during a robbery... Well,

Walt couldn't bear to think about losing a beloved uncle.

Jeffrey Lloyd, a young man Walt'd known from the one-room schoolhouse, was the shotgunner for the stagecoach on this leg of its route. It could just as easily be him that got a bullet if the Seymour gang decided to target the stagecoach.

The man in the derby hat was still watching the bank. Should Walt head over to the sheriff's office now and let his brother know about the shady character?

He glanced over his shoulder. He could see his sister's shadow through the glass window of the dressmaker's shop. Pa trusted him to keep his sister and cousins safe.

While he was vacillating, bootsteps thumped down the boardwalk nearby.

"That you, Walt? How you doing, partner?"

Tom approached from the direction of the livery. He'd seen the new ranch hand in town last Sunday, when his family had come in for church services. They hadn't had a chance to talk then.

"What're you doing in town this time of day?"

Tom's smile faltered for only a second. "Boss sent me to fetch some supplies."

Walt couldn't remember now which ranch his new friend had hired on with. He didn't want to be rude and ask again.

Tom looked up at the storefront and raised his eyebrows. "What're *you* doing here?"

Walt wished he had a better answer. "Ma asked me to bring my sister to town. Can't figure how she can spend hours shopping for one dress."

A big smile spread on Tom's face. "This the same sister who was sitting next to you in the wagon on Sunday?"

When Walt nodded, Tom swaggered over to the window and peered inside. "Does she need a second opinion?"

There was nothing salacious about the statement, just an honest appreciation. Walt shook his head with a huff. "Believe me, you do not want to go in there."

He glanced across the street to see Derby Hat Man had disappeared. Walt pivoted on his heel, looking both ways down the street. The man was nowhere in sight.

"What's wrong?" Tom asked. "You lose something?"

Walt sighed. "No. Someone was standing across the street. Looked like he was watching the bank."

Tom's brows went up, showing his skepticism. "Why would anybody do that?"

It showed the difference between them. Walt had been instantly suspicious, while Tom thought nothing of it. Tom was an ordinary citizen. Why would he worry? Walt was born to be a lawman. Instinct was important. How often had he heard Matty say that?

"There's this gang that might be hanging around the county," Walt said, taking care to keep his voice low. "The Seymour gang. Ever heard of them?"

Tom's eyes widened. "No."

"They're vicious. Robbed banks and stages and always leave a bloody mess behind."

Tom looked more serious than Walt had ever seen. His ready smile was gone. "And you think they're here? In dinky ol' Bear Creek?"

Walt thought back to Matty's words the night before. He'd told Jonas as a warning, wanting to make sure Pa kept a lookout for suspicious characters traveling through. There were a lot of women and children on the homestead. They'd be vulnerable if a gang of killers surprised them.

But Matty had also asked Jonas to keep the warning private. Walt wasn't supposed to have overheard.

So he shrugged. "Probably not."

Tom glanced at the bank, sized it up. Then he smiled an easy smile. "Bank seems pretty small. Hardly worth the trouble, huh?"

Walt looked at the bank building. He'd been in to visit his uncle when he was just a tot. He'd thought the fancy furnishings were amazing, and his uncle had let him play with his silver-plated pen.

It didn't matter if the bank was smaller than one in a big city. It was part of Walt's family legacy, and he wasn't going to let it be a casualty of the Seymour gang.

It seemed like everyone had showed up for the Founder's Day picnic. Everyone was spread out on the picnic grounds just outside of the town proper.

The women and girls wore their finery. The basket auction would be later, the proceeds going to buy new hymnals for the church. Walt's brothers had been talking about the sharpshooter competition all day.

About as long as Walt had been feeling itchy.

Like something bad was going to happen.

Things had been quiet around town ever since Walt had overheard his brother talking about the Seymour gang.

It was driving Walt crazy.

He'd thought for sure the man he'd spied skulking around the bank had been bad news. But when he'd told Matty his suspicions, his older brother had dressed him down. He'd spared no thought for Walt's feelings as he'd told him he was seeing danger where none existed, and he'd been reading too many dime novels.

Walt's pride had taken a beating. He hadn't spoken to his brother since, and it'd been two weeks.

He'd taken to scouring every newspaper he could get his hands on for news. The Seymour gang was lying low. They'd gone a month without being seen or heard from.

Walt knew it was only a matter of time before they struck again. In Bear Creek or somewhere else.

Now, he stood at the edge of the crowd, not in the mood to shake hands or rub elbows with folks in town, not when his own family still thought he was a little kid whose concerns ought to be brushed aside. Why wouldn't Matty take him seriously?

If Walt'd been in charge of the sheriff's department, he would've had extra men deputized for this event. At least two patrolling around town, where every business was empty and locked up.

A day when everyone was distracted would be the perfect time to break into the bank.

Except no one cared what Walt thought.

If Matty wasn't going to listen, that made it Walt's responsibility to watch over the town.

He left the noisy picnic grounds behind and strode down the empty boardwalk. It was so empty, it was almost eerie.

Tom stepped out of the alley beside the livery, startling Walt and making him pull up short.

"Thought you were shooting in the sharpshooter competition." Tom's voice was jovial and warm, and it called a responding smile from Walt. "If not that, I thought for sure you'd be wooing some church-going girl. Maybe bid on a basket at the auction."

Walt shook his head. "I got a funny feeling."

Tom crunched his brows together. "You need to find an outhouse?"

Walt slugged the other man's shoulder. "No. My gut's screaming that the Seymour gang is in town, but I can't get anyone to listen to me."

Tom stared past Walt's shoulder, his eyes narrowing slightly. "Seems like everybody's taking the Seymours for granted." This time when he smiled, there was a glint in his eyes that Walt didn't recognize. "Except for you."

Walt tried to see over his friend's shoulder, looking toward the bank. Everything was quiet on the boardwalk, but was that a shadow moving in the next alley over?

"How'd you get a day off to come into town for the social?" he asked.

Tom smiled easily. "Beller's foreman likes me. Is your sister selling a basket in the auction? Maybe I want to go over there and bid."

Walt laughed outright. "You don't want to bid on

Ida's basket. She's so stubborn she makes a mule seem like a kitten."

Walt would've thought that plenty to turn Tom off, but the other man looked even more interested.

"You know, I would like to meet your family. Why don't you introduce me?"

Walt's gut kicked hard. There was a muffled noise from down the street, but when he whirled on his heel, he couldn't see anything out of the ordinary.

"Give me five minutes. I just wanna walk down the street and back."

He started to walk past Tom, but his friend reached out and caught Walt's arm. Walt looked at Tom in surprise, only to find the other man had his pistol drawn and jammed into Walt's ribs.

"What the...?"

Every trace of good humor had disappeared from Tom's expression. "You're smart," he said. "Just not smart enough."

Walt shook his head, not understanding. His heartbeat was thundering in his ears, aware of that deadly weapon pointed at his midsection.

"I really don't wanna shoot you, so you better do exactly as I say."

It hit Walt then. Tom was one of them. A Seymour.

He didn't have to say it aloud. It seemed his realization had shown on his face. "Maybe we would've been friends in another lifetime. Though, you're too trusting for my taste."

Three men rushed out of the stagecoach office wearing bandannas over their faces.

They'd robbed the stage. Not the bank.

The men held burlap sacks. When they caught sight of Walt and Tom, they stopped short.

"I'm real sorry about this." Tom clocked Walt on the head, dropping him like a stone.

ALSO BY LACY WILLIAMS

Wind River Hearts series (historical romance)

Marrying Miss Marshal

Counterfeit Cowboy

Cowboy Pride

The Homesteader's Sweetheart

Courted by a Cowboy

Roping the Wrangler

Return of the Cowboy Doctor

The Wrangler's Inconvenient Wife

A Cowboy for Christmas

Her Convenient Cowboy

Her Cowboy Deputy

Catching the Cowgirl

The Cowboy's Honor

Winning the Schoolmarm

The Wrangler's Ready-Made Family

Christmas Homecoming

Cowboy Fairytales series (contemporary fairytale romance)

Once Upon a Cowboy

Cowboy Charming

The Toad Prince

The Beastly Princess

The Lost Princess

Kissing Kelsey

Courting Carrie

Stealing Sarah

Keeping Kayla

Melting Megan

The Other Princess

The Prince's Matchmaker

Hometown Sweethearts series (contemporary romance)

Kissed by a Cowboy

Love Letters from Cowboy

Mistletoe Cowboy

The Bull Rider

The Brother

The Prodigal

Cowgirl for Keeps

Jingle Bell Cowgirl

Heart of a Cowgirl

3 Days with a Cowboy

Prodigal Cowgirl

Soldier Under the Mistletoe

The Nanny's Christmas Wish

The Rancher's Unexpected Gift

Someone Old

Someone New

Someone Borrowed

Someone Blue (newsletter subscribers only)

Ten Dates

Next Door Santa

Always a Bridesmaid

Love Lessons

Sutter's Hollow series (contemporary romance)

His Small-Town Girl

Secondhand Cowboy

The Cowgirl Next Door

Not in a Series

Wagon Train Sweetheart (historical romance)

Printed in Great Britain
by Amazon

38313763R00148